HAL SCHICK

DIME DETECTIVE

Black Rose Writing | Texas

ISBN: 978-1-68433-277-9
PUBLISHED BY BLACK ROSE WRITING
www.blackrosewriting.com

Printed in the United States of America
Suggested Retail Price (SRP) $17.95

Dime Detective is printed in Calluna

To Clare and Paul
and to the memory of Howard Berk

DIME

DETECTIVE

The story takes place in the summer of 1944, when the U.S. was at war. Allied Forces had just invaded France. For Americans on the home front, government rationing was a fact of life, gasoline cost twenty cents per gallon, and pulp magazines featuring intrepid detectives were popular...

ONE

Wailing sirens pierced the hot summer night as two squad cars weaved through sparse Los Angeles traffic. With a squeal of brakes, both vehicles skidded over the curb and stopped on the sidewalk in front of an old office building on Olympic Boulevard, a couple of blocks from Central Avenue. Killing their harsh sirens, but leaving their red lights flashing, the cops emerged from their cars and approached the building's entrance. Despite the late hour, light showed from a handful of windows in the ten-story concrete structure. The chief custodian, an old-timer, who ambled about as if he had arthritis in both knees, struggled as he swung open the heavy glass door to let the police into the deserted lobby of the Chandler Building.

"You the guy phoned the police?" one of the cops asked the old man, who gamely hobbled after them.

"Yep," he said. "Been waiting on you."

"Where's the body?" the cop asked.

"On the top floor." He directed the cops to a bank of elevators and punched the UP button. "Found the guy in his own office."

"Sure he's dead?" the cop asked as the doors opened with a ding. One cop remained in the lobby, while the other three boarded the elevator along with the gimpy custodian.

"Dead as a department store dummy," the custodian said, looking around like a vaudeville comic waiting for a laugh. When all he got from the cops were a couple of tired smiles, he shrugged and pushed the button for number ten. The doors closed, and the elevator shuddered as it started upward.

"What time did you find the body?" another cop asked.

"Maybe half an hour ago when I was making my rounds."

The cop checked his watch. "That must of been about 2 A.M. Touch anything, Eddie?" he asked, glancing at the nametag on the custodian's baggy orange uniform.

"Just the door handles and, of course, the guy's telephone. The receiver was dangling by the cord over the side of the desk. I picked it up and dialed the police station. Then I told my cleaning crew to skip the dead guy's office so they wouldn't disturb the crime scene."

"You're on the ball, Eddie," the cop said wearily. "When did you punch in last night?"

"Me and my crew always get here at ten. That's when the security guard locks the lobby door. Then he's off duty. He would of mentioned it if he saw something suspicious."

"What about the elevator man?"

"Don't have one. Guess management figures that's a luxury we don't need. Especially since the elevators are out of order half the time." The elevator bumped to a stop at the tenth floor. After the doors lurched open, the custodian led his guests down the dimly lit corridor. Some of the neon ceiling lights were sputtering or burned out. Small-time businesses rented office space on the floor. They strolled past doors with stenciled or painted signs advertising a variety of goods and services: Flickinger's Rare Coins and Stamps, Wanda's Wigs and Toupees, and Dr. Fenton's Discount Dental Services.

"I can personally recommend Dr. Fenton," the old man said, a smile proudly exposing his large chalk-white choppers. "And Wanda's got rugs you can't tell from the real thing," he bragged as he patted his jet-black hairpiece, which was about as inconspicuous as a fedora on a chimpanzee.

The cops laughed and Eddie's face reddened. He stopped in front of the next door. Jingling his keys, he searched for one that fit the lock. "The light was on and the door was unlocked when I went in earlier. I locked it before I came down to wait on you fellas. Can't be too careful, you know. I'm too close to retirement for this shit to happen. I don't want no repercussions from management for messing up."

"If you can somehow manage to get the damn door open, Eddie, we'll take over from here, and you can get back to your broom," an impatient cop said as the janitor fumbled with the keys. The name stenciled on the translucent pane of glass in the top half of the door was Craven Investigations. "Don't tell me the dead guy was a gumshoe," the same cop said with a smirk.

Eddie nodded. "He's had an office here about four or five years. That's kinda long, considering a lot of these businesses are fly-by-night operations. Hear he did divorce work. Ran into him sometimes when he was working late but never had any need for his services." When Eddie finally pushed the door open, a buzzer sounded. "That noisemaker was supposed to let him know when he had a visitor. Don't think he had too many lately."

The cops quietly filed into a small waiting room and then through an open doorway into a slightly larger office. That's where they found my body—sprawled on the floor in front of my desk.

TWO

Eddie's one-liner may not have been a hit with the cops, but at least it was accurate. I *was* as dead as a department store dummy. He was wrong, however, about just touching the door handles and the office phone. The sneaky bastard went through my pockets as I lay helplessly on my back, and he lifted a twenty from my wallet. Somehow he resisted taking my last two dollars. One more thing: the number of years I'd rented office space here was actually seven, obviously not my lucky number. But why worry about such minor details at a time like this?

Lounging around the office, the prowl-car boys speculated about my killing and traded morbid comments at my expense. "Might of been an unsatisfied customer who done it," one cop said. "Or maybe a jealous dame. I hear some broads really got the hots for private eyes."

"Definitely not good for business," another noted. "Kinda looks awkward for a detective agency if the boss turns up dead at the office."

"My guess is this was a one-man operation," the third cop said. "From the looks of this dump, he was about to go under. Now the guy can't even have a going-out-of-business sale."

They departed for the lobby shortly after the detective from Central Homicide, medical examiner, police photographer, and fingerprint man showed up to start the official investigation. A reporter from the *Mirror*, a popular scandal sheet, was detained momentarily by the cop posted in the lobby. After slipping the cop a five to look the other way, the reporter, who was wearing a neck brace, was then rebuffed when he attempted to board a waiting elevator car.

"Use the fire stairs," the cop said. "And I didn't see your fat ass in case anyone wants to know." Grumbling to himself, the overweight reporter shambled over to the stairs and started his long climb to the top floor.

Meanwhile, Nick Drayton, the homicide detective, removed my wallet from my suit coat. He already knew me. He was a cop just doing his job. Drayton studied my driver's license and gun permit before taking a long look at my private investigator's license. "Expired two weeks ago," he said to no one in particular as he flipped through the rest of the wallet. "Looks like the Dime Detective finally bit off more than he could chew, and only two dollars to show for it." He frowned and shook his head.

After conferring with the medical examiner, who had just determined that my pulse and respiration were nonexistent, Drayton took out a small notebook and with a pencil stub wrote: "Sidney Craven. White male. Forty-five. Bullet wound to head. Pronounced dead at scene by ME."

"Any guess as to time of death?" Drayton asked the doctor, whose coughing and labored breathing—probably symptoms of emphysema—interrupted his reply at about every other word.

"I'd say sometime yesterday evening." The ME lifted my arm. When he let go, it fell slowly back to the floor. "Maybe between five and ten. Rigor's been at work for a while. Remember, we're not dealing with a precise science here." By the end of his little speech, he was gasping for air. One consolation of being dead: I wouldn't get hit with a debilitating disease.

"Probably a small caliber, don't you think?" Drayton was looking at my forehead, just above my wide-open eyes. "Maybe a .25 or .32. I mean the bullet didn't make a big hole. There's only a trickle of blood and no exit wound."

The ME nodded as he offered Drayton a cigarette and then lit one himself. He took a deep drag and exhaled the smoke with a sickening wheeze.

"Hell of a way to spend a Friday night," Drayton said, shaking his head.

"You mean for him or us?" the ME asked, chuckling.

"We should all be sleeping right now, not just him." The detective nodded in my direction. Yawning, he began slowly walking around the room, presumably looking for clues.

Flashbulbs popped as the police photographer began taking shots of the crime scene from different angles. Another homicide guy showed up and began chalking a yellow line around my body. He was making an outline that would remain after the corpse was carted off to the morgue.

The *Mirror* reporter finally made his entrance. He was soaked with sweat and winded from his long climb up the stairs. When he barged into the crowded office, he almost knocked over the fingerprint man, who was examining the door handle.

Pausing to catch his breath, the reporter, Bert Brenley, another acquaintance of mine, poised a pencil over his notebook and prepared to ask his usual prying questions in an effort to elicit from the homicide detective the lurid details about my untimely demise. Drayton, a shameless publicity hound, would undoubtedly cooperate. If Brenley was successful, the *Mirror* might run a huge front-page headline for his gruesome scoop about a murdered private detective.

But why get the story secondhand from a cheap, tawdry tabloid when you can get the unvarnished truth from the victim himself? There was only one place to start: at the beginning.

THREE

On a Friday afternoon, two weeks earlier, I'd just returned from a long lunch at my favorite coffee house and was pounding out a page of crime fiction on my Underwood. After reading over my lame effort, I snatched the paper from the typewriter, balled it up and winged it towards the wastebasket next to my filing cabinets. It traveled halfway around the metal rim and settled inside with the countless others that had preceded it. I took a nip from the office bottle and was about to roll another piece of paper into the machine when the phone rang.

"Craven Investigations," I said, lowering my voice a couple of octaves. "What can I do for you?"

"Mr. Craven, it's Nicholas Van Every, the manager at Muriel's. How would you like to earn double your daily fee for just an afternoon's work?"

"What's the catch?"

"We've been experiencing a shoplifting problem for some time now, and I'd like you to pose as a shopper in order to catch the thief."

"In a women's clothing store? I'd be as obvious as a circus clown in a Sunday choir."

"Not so, Mr. Craven. You may be surprised to learn that husbands frequently shop here for their wives. Now, are you available this afternoon?"

"That's me you see walking through your revolving door," I said and hung up, hoping I hadn't sounded desperate for work. As I leaned back in my swivel chair and stretched out my arms, the phone rang. Maybe business was finally picking up. It was Van Every again.

"Not so fast," he said. "You didn't give me a chance to explain the job requirements. As you wander around the store, ask the salesgirls for advice about different kinds of garments and about styles and sizes. You'll fit in like a typical husband. Just the two of us will know you're undercover. Treat any shoplifting suspect with discretion. We don't want to upset our high-society clientele." He paused, and then added, "In the future, we may be able to utilize your expertise on a regular basis." He hung up the phone.

I had located Van Every's runaway daughter earlier in the year, and he'd appreciated my discreet handling of the case. Fifty bucks for walking the floor of his glitzy store and kibitzing with the attractive salesgirls for a few hours was a welcome offer on a Friday.

Work for private detectives was rarely steady, and business had been slow lately. I'd handled a few divorce cases—mostly suspicious wives who wanted photos of their philandering husbands in telltale embraces with their girlfriends. It was sleazy work that usually required staking out lobbies in cheap hotels, but the money was spendable. Big cases just weren't coming my way. I'd always been forced to supplement my income by writing crime stories for pulp magazines such as *Detective Story* and *Dime Detective*. But a damn writer's block had been cramping my style for weeks. I hadn't had a reasonably profitable case or a published story in recent memory. No wonder I was behind in my office rent. I had even delayed renewing my investigator's license. I was desperate for work.

I wouldn't need my Colt .45 automatic for *this* assignment. Leaving my gun and shoulder holster in my desk drawer, I plucked my suit coat from the back of my chair and scooped my fedora off the desk. On my way out, I lowered the window, turned off the floor fan, hit the light switch, straightened my tie, and locked the office door—not necessarily in that order.

In the adjoining waiting room, I paused by the coffee table and splayed the outdated issues of *Life* and *Esquire* that had been neatly aligned by the cleaning crew last night. Now at least it looked like I might have had a visitor. Behind the table was a secondhand couch intended for clients. Needless to say, it hadn't been used recently.

FOUR

Retrieving my old but reliable Ford sedan from the parking lot behind my building on Olympic, I drove west through light traffic, eventually turning onto Crenshaw Boulevard. Then I took Wilshire into Beverly Hills, where Muriel's Elite Apparel was located. Lightning was snaking across the darkening sky, and rain was starting to fall by the time I reached my destination. I noticed the needle on my gas gauge was hovering near empty, but I'd fill up the tank after I got paid.

At precisely 2 P.M., I pushed through Muriel's revolving door. Leisurely strolling into the swank clothing store, I shook the raindrops off my hat and began my low-key prowling. I looked for suspicious shoppers as I walked the aisles. I passed by departments containing shoes, purses, jewelry, perfumes, and a variety of fancy garments—all exorbitantly priced. Muriel's glitzy merchandise was arranged on display tables, under glass counters, and hanging from clothes racks. The customers were mostly young and middle-aged women. Perhaps they were on a shopping spree to pick up something showy for the coming weekend.

I chatted amiably with a couple of salesgirls but moved on when I was unable to obtain their phone numbers. I found myself lingering in the lingerie section, absently fingering a black lace nightgown as I eyed a nearby salesgirl and tried to picture how the flimsy garment would look on her. My reverie was interrupted when a shopper in the next aisle caught my eye. She was wearing dark glasses, an unbuttoned blue raincoat, and a matching wide-brimmed hat. The woman plucked a red blouse from a hanger, briefly inspected it, and stuck it back on the clothes rack. Drifting along to a display table covered with an assortment of neatly arranged undergarments, she nonchalantly wadded up a brassiere in each hand and stuffed them into her coat pockets. Next, the woman pocketed a pair of black nylons. When she furtively glanced up to see me watching her every move, she spun around and hurried towards the back of the store.

"May I help you, sir?"

I turned to see a tall salesgirl looking over my shoulder. "There's no price tag on this item," I said, holding up the fancy nightgown.

"Please, try not to wrinkle the garment," she said. "I can get you a price if you're really interested."

"Why don't you model it for me?" I smoothed out the nightgown and handed it to the girl. "If I like what I see, I might buy it for you."

"You probably couldn't afford it at half off," she said, snorting.

Wincing at her stinging rejoinder, I excused myself and quickly pursued my shoplifting suspect through the store. Closing the gap between us, I stepped right in front of her just as we entered the hallway where the restrooms were located.

"Just what do you think you're doing?" she asked huffily.

"I'm a private detective," I said calmly. "You've been caught in the act of shoplifting."

"That's an outrageous lie!" she practically shrieked. "You must be deranged!" She suddenly slapped my face, knocking off my fedora. Being a lefty, she'd caught me by surprise. As I backed away, I stepped on my hat and almost went down on the recently waxed floor. While I was off balance, she hoisted a nicely shaped leg and kicked me in the groin. Howling, I doubled over in extraordinary pain. When I looked around and saw Van Every and the tall salesgirl rapidly approaching, I attempted to straighten up.

"This pervert molested me!" the woman screamed. "So I kicked him where it hurts."

"Please, let's keep our voices down," Van Every said softly, as he joined us. The manager was a thin, middle-aged man with a thick mustache and a natural frown.

"Call the cops!" she hollered, obviously ignoring his directive.

"We can clear this up if you just look in her coat pockets," I managed to say between groans while I leaned against the wall next to the LADIES door. Curious shoppers were wandering over for a closer look.

"Don't you *dare* lay a hand on me," she said as Van Every took half a step towards her. With a flair for the dramatic, she suddenly opened her raincoat to reveal her undone blouse. The shrewd bitch must have yanked it open while I was bent in agony. "See what that bastard did!" she screeched while looking at Van Every and wagging a long-nailed finger at me. "I should sue this store for allowing him on the premises. I could cause plenty of trouble. If you think I'm bluffing, just try me. I'm Simone Pearson, the actress, and I've got connections." When she noticed Van Every and me leering at her exposed cleavage, she quickly covered up with her raincoat and glared at us with disdain.

"I beg your pardon, Miss Pearson," Van Every said obsequiously, "but I didn't recognize you."

"For your information, I often do my shopping incognito. Otherwise, the unwanted attention would just wear me out." She started sobbing loudly.

"Please, remain calm. We don't want to alarm our other customers."

"You mean the *paying* customers?" I said.

"Mr. Van Every, I saw this disgusting man fondling a sexy nightgown with his sweaty hands before he followed Miss Pearson to the back of the store." The lingerie salesgirl had just landed the knockout blow in our little altercation.

Apologizing profusely, the store manager offered the shoplifter a hundred-dollar gift certificate, a gesture she declined by just shaking her head. "Perhaps you'd like a free umbrella," he said. "The weatherman's calling for rain." Van Every plucked an umbrella from a nearby display stand, twirled it in the air, caught it, and presented it to the actress. Unimpressed with Van Every's apparent attempt to lighten the mood, she snatched the umbrella from his hand and departed in a huff.

As she clacked through the store in her high heels, I attempted to tell my side to Van Every, but he just shook his head in disbelief. He took out his wallet, extracted a fifty, and briskly handed it to me.

"We won't be needing your services anymore today," he said scornfully.

"Does that mean I won't be able to use you as a reference?" I responded with a sneer. "Contrary to Miss Pearson's claim, I never touched the wacky dame. She attacked *me*. You should have checked her pockets. I believe an inventory of your store's undergarments will exonerate me and indicate you've been duped."

"Please leave quietly, Craven, or I'll call the police."

"Don't I get an umbrella?"

Van Every pointed towards the revolving door. I pocketed the fifty and picked up my deformed hat, poking it back into shape. It was a huge store and a long walk to the door. The commotion had caught the attention of a growing number of nosy bystanders. Trying to ignore their whispering and finger-pointing, I made my exit. On the way, I glimpsed a twitchy brunette discreetly pocket a colorful scarf. Apparently Simone Pearson hadn't been the only shoplifter on the premises. Now, thanks to the distraction I was providing, *this* thief could operate with impunity.

When I finally shouldered my way through the revolving door, I was greeted by a raging thunderstorm. Rain pelted me like fistfuls of bullets flung by some heartless prankster for the amusement of the snooty audience watching my plight from behind Muriel's plate glass windows. Dignity wouldn't permit my returning to the shelter of the store, and my clothes were quickly drenched. I rejected the notion of making a crude gesture at the gawking shoppers and, instead, flamboyantly doffed my hat and began dancing like a hoofer in a movie musical. Sufficiently recovered from my earlier trouncing, I improvised a sequence of lively dance steps as I splashed through several puddles on my way down the sidewalk, which I had all to myself thanks to the storm. A couple of nearly disastrous stumbles upset my rhythm, but I somehow managed to remain upright. Once I'd made it beyond the store windows, I dashed for the parking lot and the refuge of my awaiting vehicle.

Although out of breath when I reached my Ford, I had regrouped and was ready for the weekend, the start of which was briefly delayed when I discovered my car was out of gas. That didn't rankle me for more than a minute. After all, I had just made fifty bucks and was already as soaked as I was going to get. I trudged to the nearest filling station, talked the attendant into the loan of a gas can, and handed him some pocket change for the gallon of fuel he pumped into the container. My mood only slightly dampened, I returned to my vehicle. By then the rain had slackened. After tossing the empty can into my trunk, I drove over to my apartment building on Alvarado Street.

I hung up my drenched brown suit in the closet. It would be dry and ready for whatever job might come my way on Monday. I changed into my blue backup suit. Purchased on sale, it was a size too large, but at least it wasn't sopping wet. Suddenly hungry, I drove to a nearby Chinese takeout place and returned home for a quick dinner. Following a long nap, I was off to my favorite watering hole, the Twilight Lounge, an almost respectable hangout on Sunset Boulevard.

FIVE

Drifting into the smoky, dimly lit joint, I casually gave it the once-over before selecting a barstool next to a gorgeous redhead, who—at least momentarily—was alone. I folded up the soggy newspaper I'd used to deflect the rain as I walked from my car and dropped it on the floor under my seat. Then I placed my hat on the bar top, loosened my tie, took out my pack of Chesterfields, and lit my last one.

"Buy you a drink?" I asked, noticing the redhead's glass was nearly empty. She took a drag from her cigarette and, exhaling, slowly turned my way. Raising her eyebrows, she gave me a quick look before returning, with a careless shrug, to her drink.

"Suit yourself." She drained the dregs from her glass.

"Hey, Danny," I said, waving my fifty at the bartender. "How about some service?" The bill's denomination caught the redhead's attention—just as I figured—and she leaned close to me.

"I'd like another rum and Coke," she whispered in my ear. "That is if it's all right with you."

"The usual for me," I told Danny, "and the lady wants another one." After making her drink and pouring me a whiskey, he snatched my fifty off the counter.

"So, what brings you out to the Twilight Lounge on a night like this?" I said. "Have a fight with your boyfriend?"

"I was supposed to meet someone here. But it looks like I got stood up."

"Well, his loss is my gain," I said with a smile. "I'm Sidney."

"I'm Ginger." She placed her hand gently on my arm just as Danny slipped my change onto the bar. My smile faded when I noticed three singles and two quarters sitting in front of me.

"Danny, my man, I gave you a fifty—not a five."

"Right you are, Mr. Craven. I just settled your bar tab for you. We've been carrying you for months. Now we're even. I was beginning to wonder if you'd *ever* pay up. The owner's gonna be happy. He's been after me to crack down on freeloaders." Danny chuckled softly as he sauntered towards the other end of the bar.

"Damn it," I said under my breath. Ginger's hand was no longer on my sleeve, and she was swiveling on her barstool while casually gazing around the packed joint. I tried to think of a witty line that would hold her attention.

"Excuse me, Sid," she said, standing up, "but I just spotted an old friend. Thanks for the drink." She jabbed her cigarette in an ashtray and left the butt smoldering. With her drink in one hand, her purse in the other, and an umbrella hooked over her arm, Ginger waltzed over to a corner table. Wearing a tight yellow dress, she had a figure that could easily inspire the pope to renounce celibacy. My excellent view of her swaying backside, however, was spoiled when I found myself trying to blink away the smoke spiraling up from her carelessly discarded cigarette. She joined a soldier, who had been sitting by himself, and they were soon chatting in voices that carried above the din.

"Who's the overweight guy at the bar?" the GI asked, snickering. "Your dad or your uncle?"

"Never seen him before," Ginger said. "Looks like he slept in his clothes. Not to mention the big splotch on his tie." They both laughed.

I looked around the bar to see if I could identify the object of their contempt. I chuckled to myself when I saw the obese guy slouched on a barstool on the other side of Ginger's empty seat. He was Bert Brenley, a Hollywood reporter I'd run into occasionally. He had to be close to fifty. With his numerous chins, he looked like he'd swallowed a stack of pancakes. Next to him was some sweet young number, probably a starlet hoping to get mentioned in his tabloid gossip column. Guess she would do anything for a little publicity. Glancing at Brenley, I thought it was shameful how some people could just let themselves go. After one last drag, I stubbed out my cigarette, then finished my drink and scooped up my change. I'd leave a tip next time.

I got on my feet and with some difficulty tucked in my shirt. While brushing the wrinkles from my clothes, I noticed a spot on my tie. How the hell did that get there? Then I remembered the takeout chow mien I had downed earlier. With a sigh, I donned my hat. As I exited the joint, I nodded at Ginger, but she didn't seem to notice.

I'd pick up a fifth of whiskey and some smokes on the way home. I could still drink my troubles away but at half the cost.

SIX

After a rainy weekend, Monday arrived with blue skies and a pleasant breeze. Suffering from a sizable hangover, I walked into my office about nine. As I opened the window to relieve the musty odor, the phone began to ring. Some rich guy's butler wondered if I might be interested in handling a case for his employer. Answering in the affirmative, I was given an address and a time: 10 A.M. sharp.

"Could you tell me what the case is about?" I asked.

"I'm sure Mr. McGahee will fill you in adequately," he responded with a touch of scorn in his voice.

"Can't you just give me a hint?" What I got was a dial tone. I wasn't about to have my leisurely morning routine wrecked by some snotty butler. I decided to make a couple of phone calls. Barhopping over the weekend, I had talked two girls into giving me their phone numbers, which I'd scribbled on the back of a business card. I dialed the numbers, but both turned out to be bogus.

Taking an occasional sip from the office bottle, I casually sorted out the mail that had been delivered after I'd left on Friday. I opened a letter from my literary agent, Morris Provost, who wanted to know if I had written any new detective fiction. Morrie had helped me get started in the business. He'd sold dozens of my short stories to pulp magazines before I ran out of ideas. In his familiar scribble, he encouraged me to keep writing. He said I'd eventually hit my stride again. Morrie's alimony payments to two ex-wives, the mortgage payments on his luxury home, and his faraway vacations had driven him to the brink of bankruptcy. He missed his fifteen percent. I folded his letter into a paper airplane and sailed it out the window.

My landlord had mailed me a warning notice in large print regarding my overdue office rent. I glanced at my wall calendar, courtesy of Wanda, my neighbor down the hallway. She thought it would brighten up my bleak office. The June picture featured a leggy model ostensibly in one of Wanda's wigs. Wearing a sexy swimsuit, she was reclining poolside. The calendar was promoting wigs—not swimsuits—but who could tell? The caption read: "New summer styles and more for 1944."

I managed to find today's date: the nineteenth. I was less than three weeks behind on my rent. During my seven years in this shabby building, I'd had my ups and downs. I had been tardy before but had always caught up. Being a long-time tenant would buy me some time. I balled up the notice and heaved it across the room. It bounced off the side of my filing cabinet and into the wastebasket.

I found an advertisement for a comprehensive manual on the science of tailing suspects. One section supposedly offered advice for a detective who gets spotted by the suspect he's tailing and then finds himself tailed by the suspect. There was more to read, but I didn't want to amplify my headache. The cost of the manual was ten bucks. I shuffled all the ads together and discarded them before finally heading over to McGahee's.

After ringing the doorbell, I stepped back and glanced down at my shoes. Then I plucked a handkerchief from the coat pocket of my slightly rumpled brown suit. I bent over and polished my dusty wing tips.

"What can I do for you?"

I looked up to see the butler sternly scrutinizing me as he swung the door open. He was an elderly fellow but looked reasonably fit in his dark suit. I straightened up and tucked my handkerchief back into my pocket. "I'm here to see Mr. McGahee."

"Who shall I say is calling?" he inquired loftily.

"You may say Mr. Craven is calling," I replied with a pompous tone of my own. "I have an appointment."

"For what time?"

"Ten," I said, glancing at my watch. "Okay, so I'm a little late."

"May I see a business card?"

"Why not?" I took out my wallet, and with a flourish I removed a dog-eared card and handed it over. Holding it at arm's length by one corner as if it might be toxic, he disappeared into the house and closed the door. It was ten-thirty. I was a half-hour late for my appointment with Vincent McGahee. Now it was my turn to wait, but I didn't mind. I paced back and forth on the brick walkway leading to the side entrance of McGahee's gaudy two-story mansion on Beverly Glen Boulevard. It was a swanky neighborhood in the foothills north of Sunset. I lit a cigarette and hummed a tune, the title of which escaped me.

I needed a big case to get me out of the red. Maybe this was going to be it. Maybe I'd even make enough to take a faraway vacation—at least as far away as Catalina Island. I wondered if the McGahee I was about to meet was any relation to the oil magnate Victor McGahee. After striking it rich years earlier, he had become a favorite of Southern California's high society. Now he was an investment banker who ran his own company.

The butler suddenly opened the door, putting an end to my wondering. I dropped my cigarette butt, and with the sole of my shoe ground it out on McGahee's previously spotless walkway. Giving me a disapproving look, the butler beckoned me to follow him. I just smiled. I somehow sensed I was only moments away from a lucrative case and deliverance from my financial woes.

SEVEN

"This way," the butler said dismissively. I followed him down a long hallway and past a winding staircase that led to the second floor. We stepped into a spacious, thickly carpeted living room crowded with antique furniture. As we made our way through, I tried in vain to identify at least one of the elaborately framed paintings adorning the walls. One picture, a bunch of polka dots of various sizes and colors, had a small bullet-sized hole in the lower corner. Maybe it was the artist's way of drawing attention to his scrawled signature, which was unreadable anyway. Maybe it was his trademark. Or maybe an art lover had taken a shot at the painting. One way or the other, it was probably worth a fortune. Maybe I was in the wrong business. We continued along another hall and stopped at an open door leading to McGahee's large study.

"Your detective has arrived, sir," the butler said and then promptly departed.

"Come in, Mr. Craven, and make yourself comfortable," said a young, dark-haired man sitting at a desk facing a bay window in the only wall not covered with bookshelves. While McGahee shuffled papers, I took a glance out the window. A variety of trees and neatly trimmed bushes surrounded a bright-green lawn. I removed my hat and selected a luxurious easy chair near the center of the room. When he suddenly swung around, I noticed he was in a wheelchair. He couldn't have been more than thirty. He was wearing fancy pajamas, a monogrammed lounging robe, and slippers.

"I'm Vincent McGahee," he said. "Being a detective, you probably already figured that out." I smiled politely while he chuckled and took a long look at his watch. "I'm pressed for time," he added, "so let's skip the small talk."

"Okay by me," I said agreeably.

"Have you handled many missing persons cases?"

"That's my specialty," I said. Who didn't exaggerate sometimes? I nonchalantly tossed my hat onto a nearby couch and was about to reach for a smoke, but I couldn't find an ashtray anywhere.

"My wife is missing," he said. "I'd like you to find her."

"When's the last time you saw her?"

"Thursday night. Let's see." His eyes darted around the room as if he were gathering details. "We went to bed about ten. My medication always knocks me out. When I woke up Friday morning she was gone. I just assumed she went to work. But it turned out she never showed up. She was seen around town later on Friday." He looked at me. "Then she took a powder."

"Who saw her on Friday?"

"*You* did, Mr. Craven." He raised his eyebrows. "Don't tell me you don't remember bumping into my wife."

"I don't believe I've ever had that pleasure," I said, bewildered. My lingering hangover wasn't helping my memory any.

"Do you think it's just by chance that you're here?" He smirked. "A reliable source told me you were one of the last people to see her before she disappeared."

"Oh!" I smiled as my memory flickered into focus. "You mean the redhead at the Twilight Lounge on Friday night. Why didn't you say so in the first place?"

"At Muriel's, Mr. Craven, in the afternoon," he said impatiently. "My wife is Simone Pearson. She uses her own name. She's an actress. And she's a blonde."

I suddenly felt like I was drowning in the cushy chair. Remaining calm, I managed to free myself. "The police have the manpower it takes for tracking down missing persons." I took a step towards the door. "That's your best bet."

"Hold on, Mr. Craven." He started to propel his wheelchair forward, and for a minute I thought he was going to cut off my retreat. He stopped after rolling only a couple of feet. "You have every right to be upset. Mr. Van Every phoned me from Muriel's and told me all about the unfortunate episode at his store. Sorry you got caught in the middle. Apparently he was concerned that I might sue him. He apologized umpteen times for the misunderstanding."

"*What* misunderstanding?" I demanded. "Your wife's accusation against me was completely fabricated. She's the one who assaulted *me*. I caught her red-handed."

"I'm on *your* side, Mr. Craven. You wouldn't be here if I didn't believe you. It's not the *only* time my wife was collared for shoplifting and then threw a tantrum. But the charges were always dropped, and I managed to keep her name out of the papers."

"Did you clear *my* name with Van Every? Did you tell him your wife went haywire?"

"I'm trying to protect my wife. So I wasn't about to question Mr. Van Every's version of the incident. Besides, it's your word against Simone's, and she's not available for comment. Van Every could have called the police, but luckily he wants to avoid publicity. Mr. Craven, the two of us know the truth. You'll just have to take this one on the chin." When I started to object, he raised both hands to silence me. "Don't worry, I intend to make it worth your while. Let me get you a drink," he said as if offering me a bribe.

If I walked out now, I'd be jobless again with no prospects in sight. What did I have to lose? Reluctantly, I decided to stick around and listen to the rest of his story. "A whiskey would be much appreciated." With a sigh, I settled back into that addictive easy chair.

"Geoffrey!" McGahee yelled. The butler appeared almost immediately, pushing a cart containing assorted bottles of booze. After pouring us both a drink, he departed as quietly as a peeping Tom.

"Okay if I smoke?" I asked. He nodded, and I got an ashtray from the drink cart. When he declined to join me, I lit up a Chesterfield.

"One thing you should know, Mr. Craven. My wife's an alcoholic. On top of that, she's been down in the dumps ever since my injury. Even with medication I'm in pain. Guess I've been home about a month now, and, uh, we still haven't been able to sleep together. The doctors say there's a fifty-fifty chance I'll never fully recover. Or vice versa if you're the optimistic sort."

"What happened, Mr. McGahee?"

"Seven weeks ago, I was forced to crash-land my airplane after taking flak on a bombing mission over France. I'm glad to say all my crew survived. I was told the story made all the papers here."

"You were a military pilot?" I said, making a mental note to skim the newspapers more carefully in the future. My reading was generally limited to sports and crime reporting. He frowned, apparently irritated by my interruption.

"Anyway," he continued, "my fuselage was heavily damaged and my landing gear disabled. I was lucky to make it back to friendly territory. A number of my toes got blown off by shrapnel, and my legs are partially paralyzed. I've got to learn how to walk all over again. I spent a few weeks in a military hospital in London where I underwent treatment, but there wasn't much they could do for me. Now, I have daily therapy sessions with a nurse." McGahee looked frustrated. "As far as I'm concerned, my war wounds are ancient history. I want my wife back!" He shook his fist.

"When were you married?" I asked offhandedly.

"We got married in December 1941. It was the day before Pearl Harbor was attacked. Like countless other good Americans, I joined up a couple days later. After a two-week honeymoon, we moved into this house, which was a wedding gift from my father. All too soon I was off to basic training and flight school. We didn't have much time together before I was sent overseas."

"By any chance, does Victor McGahee happen to be your father?" I couldn't resist asking.

"None other than the oil tycoon himself."

"You could hire a big detective agency. Why choose *me* for the job?"

"I got your name from Van Every. He didn't exactly recommend you. But I figured, since you saw my wife just the other day, you would have a head start in finding her. You know what she looks like in person, and you actually talked to her."

"It wasn't much of a conversation. Why do you think she'd resort to shoplifting, anyway? You could buy her all the clothes she wants, even at Muriel's excessive prices."

"Now, I'm not a psychiatrist," he said with a shrug, "but I think Simone's shoplifting is a reaction to my confinement in a wheelchair."

"Huh?"

"I'm unable to give Simone the attention she craves, and so she seeks it elsewhere. She shoplifts in order to get caught, in order to be the center of attention."

"But she's an actress. She's already in the spotlight."

"Mr. Craven, if you were a movie fan you'd know my wife's career has gone into a tailspin. Simone hasn't had a big hit in some time. She was supposed to begin a new film on Friday. It would have been her first movie role in months, but she was a no-show at the studio. Since I've been back, Simone's been moody and unstable, as you found out for yourself. She was spending her days sulking around the house, drinking, and taking all sorts of pills. I was the one who encouraged her to get back in front of the camera, but I guess she just couldn't handle it."

"How long has your wife had a drinking problem?" I took a gulp of my whiskey.

"Simone always had a taste for alcohol. But her drinking got out of hand while I was overseas. Did I mention she got sacked by her studio earlier this year? I heard rumors the reason was because of her drinking. I think she got in with the wrong crowd. My father tried to watch over her while I was gone, but he's a busy man. Just before I came home she was arrested for drunken driving. He didn't know what to do with her. He took her to a revival meeting in Echo Park. Some female evangelist put the fear of God in her. She sobered up for a while but started drinking again a few days after my return."

"What about other family members? Didn't they try to help her?"

"Simone's parents are deceased. And *my* mother died some years ago. Simone's younger sister, Ashley, has been staying here with us for a couple weeks. Simone phoned her after one of her drinking binges. She'd spent a night in some cheap hotel. Wouldn't tell me where. She returned the next day with a severe hangover. Ashley took the train down from her home in San Francisco. At first, I was opposed to the idea. But she's been providing moral support for Simone and helping her cope with her alcoholism. With her sister's help, she's been on the wagon for about a week. But now it looks like..."

He hesitated and sipped his drink. "You're welcome to speak with Ashley, but she took my car downtown on an errand. My father got me a 1942 Buick to celebrate my return home. You know, that was the last year they made new cars before the government shut down production. They've been stockpiling those vehicles. I have no idea how he was able to get his hands on one. Of course I can't drive it now. Maybe someday."

Frowning, he grabbed a newspaper from his desk. "Have you seen today's *Times*?"

I shook my head. I'd neglected to stop by the newsstand this morning. He held up the paper and pointed to the headline on the front page.

"Shouldn't detectives keep up on city crime?" he said. "Another young actress was found dead in her apartment. A victim of the Starlet Strangler. That makes four in about four weeks. Maybe Simone fell into the clutches of this madman."

"How old is your wife?"

"She's thirty-five, ten years older than me."

"And how long has she been in movies?"

"Guess about twelve years."

"All the dead girls were in their early twenties and just starting out in showbiz. You know, starlets. They were single and living alone. I don't think the strangler got Simone." I had been following the sensational case and knew the killer's habits. His victims were found choked to death in their apartments but otherwise unmolested. Apparently the only evidence the guy left behind was the fingerprints on the necks of his prey.

"Just thought I'd ask," he said, flipping the paper back on his desk.

"How did your wife spend Thursday, the day before she vanished?"

"She went to Empire Studios for a rehearsal of her new movie. She was anxious to prove she was worthy of getting another chance. Apparently everything went okay."

"But then things fell apart on Friday," I said.

"It started when her studio called, wanting to know where she was. Then Van Every phoned with more bad news. I waited up with her sister till after midnight. We were hoping to hear her pull into the driveway. But after she left Muriel's, Simone just dropped out of sight." He took a deep breath and exhaled slowly.

"What make of car does she drive?" I asked.

"She's got a green Packard convertible."

"She didn't happen to take a suitcase full of clothes with her, did she?"

"I'm one step ahead of you. I already checked, and everything's still in her closet."

"Maybe your servants know something, Mr. McGahee."

"You've met the butler. Geoffrey comes in weekdays and the maid twice a week. Nothing like having servants, especially when you're an invalid. The butler's a new addition since my return from overseas. He's on loan from my father." He paused. "Simone was gone when Geoffrey got here Friday morning, and Juanita had the day off."

"Who'd you call about your wife's disappearance?"

"I didn't know *who* to call. After hearing about her run-in with you, I thought she might have gone on another drinking spree and then checked into a hotel. When I didn't hear from her by this morning, I decided to call you. We want to keep this out of the papers. My father's concerned that a scandal might tarnish the family's good name—and it could kill Simone's shot at a comeback."

"That's why you don't want the police involved."

"You're very perceptive, Mr. Craven." I pretended not to notice his mocking tone. "Now, how much are you going to cost me?"

"Twenty-five a day plus expenses."

"Would a retainer of, say, two hundred be satisfactory?"

"That'll get me started. Can I get a recent picture of your wife? And can you tell me the names of any of her acquaintances and how to get in touch with them?" I didn't see any framed photos of Simone on his desk or any other photos. He wheeled around and rummaged through his desk drawer while I stubbed out my forgotten cigarette and poured myself another drink. He found an eight-by-ten photograph, which he dropped on his desk, and then opened his checkbook and did some scribbling. Two hundred was a considerable retainer, but it might be my only income for the whole month. He spun around, wheeled over, and handed me a check along with a glossy black-and-white publicity shot of three women dressed in military uniforms. Then he wheeled backwards to his desk and picked up his drink.

"You may have seen this photo before," he said. "It was reprinted in countless newspapers across the country. That's Simone in the middle. My wife and two other actresses were doing their part to seduce new recruits into signing up with Uncle Sam. Of course, they'd probably get drafted anyway." He smiled. "The photo was taken just after we returned from our honeymoon in San Francisco. I think the other two actresses were also contract players at Empire Studios. I don't know their names, and I really have no idea where they are now. That's the best I can do for you." McGahee took a sip of his drink while I downed the rest of mine. "I've been overseas for more than two years, Mr. Craven. Things change."

I nodded as I thought about the information he'd given me. This case was definitely more complex than my typical divorce work. With some effort I got on my feet and then reached for my hat.

"I'll keep in touch," I said, walking over and extending my hand. He leaned forward, and I thought he might rise up. But after we shook, he slouched back in his wheelchair.

"Please keep a low profile, Mr. Craven."

"That's the only way I operate," I assured him. "No need to summon Geoffrey," I quickly added. "I can find my own way out." I'd had enough of that strutting butler for one day. I departed with mixed feelings. I was relieved to be working again but concerned that I didn't have much to go on. There's no way McGahee told me everything he knew. Nobody ever did.

My Ford didn't exactly fit in with the newer Buicks, Chryslers, and Caddies in the vicinity. Instead of parking in McGahee's sizable driveway, I had found a spot down the street. I didn't want to advertise my social standing. If he knew I drove a lousy secondhand car, he might think twice about hiring me. I wasn't taking any chances.

The neighborhood was too uptown for sidewalks. Pedestrians weren't welcome. I strolled along the side of the street as I studied the publicity photo of the three women in Army fatigues. Simone was seated at a desk and signing a document of some sort. She was flanked by two younger actresses leaning attentively over the desk. The camera had captured their radiant smiles. All three had nametags, but Simone's was the only one clearly visible. It said: "Private Pearson." The caption below the photo read: "Joining up is as easy as one, two, three."

Simone looked carefree in the photo, definitely unlike her counterpart in real life. What had happened to her in the two and a half years since the picture was taken? For the most part, she'd had a successful career. I had seen her in a number of films, but I couldn't recall any of the titles. Looking closely at the photo, I recognized the actress on the right. She'd played a minor part in a recent film, but I didn't know her name.

I wasn't sure where to begin my search, but I figured an idea would come to me eventually. Feeling better, I started whistling my way down the street. When I reached my car, I found a parking ticket under the wiper blade. I didn't see any signs anywhere. Maybe the cop was trying to tell me what I already knew: my old sedan didn't belong here. The same could be said of me. I crumpled up the yellow piece of paper and tossed it into the backseat. Nothing was going to darken my mood. My first stop would be the bank, then the liquor store. I'd take care of my overdue bills but not now. I was employed and that called for at least a modest celebration.

EIGHT

Late Tuesday morning, I woke up with a nasty hangover and an enormous hairball lodged in my throat. I tried to spit out the hairball until I realized it only *felt* like a hairball. Two cups of coffee later and I was ready to rejoin the civilized world. I showered, put on my brown suit and hat, and headed for Hollywood. I took Alvarado and, after turning onto Sunset, paused at Batson's Coffee House for some waffles.

I scanned the front page of today's *Times* as I waited for my order. The city was reeling from the recent discovery of the Starlet Strangler's fourth victim. The mayor had called on the newly formed strangler task force to redouble its efforts to nab the killer. Despite having no reliable eyewitnesses and little useful evidence, a police spokesman said, the cops were determined to protect Hollywood starlets and prevent more slayings.

"How about a movie tonight?" I asked my favorite waitress as she brought my waffles and refilled my coffee cup. She was a willowy brunette, about thirty, with a freewheeling style that kept my hopes alive.

"Got a previous engagement, Sid, my boy," she said.

"Cancel it. I got some serious pocket money, but it won't last forever."

"Finally landed an assignment, huh?"

"I'm talking big time, Betty, big time."

"You know, Sidney, I like your suit," she said, changing the subject, "but it would go better with a shave." Laughing, she patted my face and moved on to the next table.

I rubbed a hand over my stubble. "Go out with me and I'll grab a shave."

"Now that you got some spending money, maybe I should introduce you to my husband's sister," said Betty, returning to my table.

"There's no time like right now."

"She got divorced a couple months ago, and she's just getting back into circulation."

"A divorced woman!" I said happily. "Tell me more."

"Her name's Lucy. I'll talk to her."

"Tell her I'm a great guy—witty, good-looking, and loaded."

"No way," she said, laughing. "It'll be too much of a letdown when she meets you." Betty walked off towards the kitchen.

"Tell her..." When I realized she was already out of earshot, I glanced at the war news and started on my waffles. Allied forces had gained a solid foothold in Normandy. Some military experts predicted the war would be over within two years. When I finished my coffee, I stuck two singles under my plate and took my paper. I'd catch up on the sports news later. Or maybe I wouldn't. Baseball just wasn't the same without the famous players who had joined the military. Nowadays, I didn't recognize the names in the box scores.

Running on time for a change, I paused and tipped my hat as I passed Betty on my way out. I had known her for a number of years but had been unable to entice her into cheating on her husband, a used-car salesman. I'd seen him at Batson's a couple of times. He was a short, bald guy—just not Betty's type. But maybe his sister Lucy was *my* type.

Ten minutes later I drove up to the entrance to Empire Studios on Hollywood Boulevard. When a white-haired security guard emerged from an adjacent booth, I told him I was a private detective and gave him my name. He was wearing a neatly pressed blue uniform and carried a sidearm, which I doubted was even loaded. I'd left *my* gun at the office on Monday and hadn't been back there since. After a cursory glance at his clipboard, he notified me that I wouldn't be permitted to enter.

"As a general rule, we don't allow gumshoes on the lot," he smugly announced.

Expecting to get the brush-off, I was prepared with a reply that I figured would rock the old gentleman back on his heels, if not bring him to his knees. "I'm not just *any* private investigator." I flipped open my wallet, giving him a peek at my license. He squinted at it through thick eyeglasses. "I'm working on an important case for Vincent McGahee," I explained. "He's heir to the McGahee oil fortune."

"Looks like your license has expired," he muttered as I snatched my wallet away.

"You need new glasses," I said. "Let's get to the point. I assume you've heard the name McGahee before."

"So what if I did, sonny?" he replied in a surly tone. "You can't get through unless your name is on my list, and it ain't." He thumped his clipboard defiantly.

"Let me make it simple for you, pops. This is a missing persons case involving a well-known actress from Empire Studios. Now, I wouldn't want you to lose your job over this. Old man McGahee carries a lot of weight in this town. Why don't you just check with your boss? He'll straighten you out."

"Wait here," he said, a worried look abruptly rearranging the complex patterns of wrinkles on his leathery face. He slowly stepped back into his guard booth and picked up a telephone. Through the window, I saw him dial a number and then talk briefly into the mouthpiece. He held the phone down by his side. "Just a minute," he called out. "They put me on hold." The guard lifted up the phone again and turned his back on me.

I looked at my watch. It was almost noon. The studio's fancy wrought-iron gates had already been swung open. I engaged the clutch, eased my foot down on the gas, and drove onto the movie lot. The old man would thank me for not allowing him to detain me unnecessarily. I passed a couple of large buildings and turned into a parking area with an orange VISITORS sign. I pulled into an empty space between two shiny late-model cars and made a mental note to wash my car and give it a wax job. Assuming the movie crowd would break for lunch momentarily, I asked an extra, sauntering along in a cowboy outfit, for directions to the commissary. With any luck, I'd find one of Simone's acquaintances on lunch break. If I asked the right questions, I might get a lead on the missing woman's whereabouts.

NINE

On the way to the studio cafeteria, I was accompanied by actors and actresses—in a variety of costumes—as they emerged from movie sets and sound stages along the walkway. Pirates, prisoners, soldiers, doctors, nurses, and nuns joined the parade.

When we reached our destination, I looked around for someone who could identify the actresses next to Simone in the recruitment photo I was brandishing. I recognized a handful of famous faces among those idling in line with their trays at the food counter or assembling at tables in the huge dining area. Catching the attention of a woman dressed as a cigarette girl, I raised my voice to make my question heard over the clatter of trays and the nonstop hum of conversation.

She studied the publicity shot for a minute and then glanced around the busy commissary. "The one on the right side in your photo is over there with a hotshot director." She pointed towards a couple at a table by the wall. They were seated under an old movie poster of King Kong clutching a frantic female in his fist while standing atop the Empire State Building.

"What's her name?"

"Everyone will know her name soon enough. She's sleeping her way to the top. She's Tina Ferrante."

I reclaimed my photo from the woman, who sounded like a jealous extra waiting for *her* chance. "What movie are *you* in, honey?" I asked pleasantly.

"I work here, wise guy. Now, how about a pack of Lucky Strikes?" She plucked a package of cigarettes off a tray that was suspended from her neck by a red, white, and blue strap.

"I'm trying to quit," I said, hurrying off. My hunch that I'd run into one of the actresses in the photo had actually paid off. As I approached Tina's table, I noticed that her lanky companion, the hotshot director, had his arm draped familiarly around her shoulder. I barely recognized the actress under a blonde wig and in a flapper costume from the Roaring Twenties. He was wearing a white suit and looked about fifty. She was probably half his age. The couple, engrossed in conversation, hadn't even touched their hamburgers and fries.

"Hello, Miss Ferrante," I said, removing my hat, placing it on the table, and smoothly sliding into a chair across from them. "I'm Sidney Craven, a private detective. Pardon my interruption, but I understand you know Simone Pearson."

"Has anything happened to her?" she said, glancing at the director.

"She disappeared, and her husband's concerned about her welfare. I was wondering if you'd seen her recently."

"Funny you should ask," Tina said. "I hadn't seen her in months. Then—out of the blue—she shows up to audition for a part in a movie." She gestured towards the tall guy next to her. "This is Howard Seymour. He's the director."

Seymour reached out a large bony hand and we shook. "You say your name is Craven?" he asked.

"That's right."

"And you're a private detective? Someone who risks life and limb on dangerous cases?"

I showed him my license and then flicked my wallet shut. "What about it?"

"And you've never had any trouble drumming up business?"

"Why should I?"

"You just don't look the type. If I were casting a detective movie, I definitely wouldn't pick someone who looked like you for the part. You're not tall enough, and your shoulders aren't wide enough. You don't have that tough-guy look. Maybe if you worked out some." Seymour cracked a grin and nudged Tina with an elbow. "Just kidding around, buddy."

I forced a smile.

"Let me see if I can help you, Mr. Craven," he said. "Miss Pearson's agent sent her over for a screen test last Tuesday. An actress had just quit after getting into an argument with me about how her part should be played, and we were auditioning for a last-minute replacement. It was a small but pivotal part. I was skeptical about casting Miss Pearson in the role, but she read for me and turned out to be just what I was looking for. I hired her on the spot and gave her a copy of the screenplay so she could learn her lines." He picked up a French fry and then dropped it back on his plate.

"She came in Thursday for her rehearsal and costume fitting," he continued. "We were scheduled to shoot her first scene on Friday. But she didn't show. When we couldn't reach her by phone, the part went to Miss Ferrante, who just happened to be available. This is the second time we've had to get a replacement for that role. Now I'm falling behind schedule. It was just too much of a gamble to hire Miss Pearson."

"Why?"

"For one thing, she's been on hiatus from showbiz ever since she got bounced by Empire for suddenly taking time off during a movie shoot. She was a contract player back then. Now she gets herself an agent, and I give her a part in my movie, and she pulls the same trick." Seymour rubbed his forehead as if just talking about Simone gave him a headache. "You know, sometimes it takes a while to get back in the groove. Maybe she just wasn't ready. Rumors been floating around she's got a drinking problem." He turned to Tina.

"It must be a difficult time for her," she said, shrugging. "You know, with her husband coming back paralyzed from overseas. I ran into her the other day as we were leaving the commissary. Simone was about to start her movie and mine was about to wrap. We only had a few minutes for small talk. We reminisced about the old days when her husband was off in the war, and we'd go shopping or to a movie."

"Did you ever hear any gossip about her doing a little, uh, shoplifting?" I asked.

"Never," she said, shaking her head in disbelief. "Why *would* she? She's got money. Her father-in-law's an oil tycoon."

"For your information, I recently caught her myself while working undercover at a glitzy women's clothing store."

"Muriel's? We shopped there sometimes."

"No comment. Look, Miss Pearson's been missing since Friday. Any guess where she might be?"

The two shook their heads in unison. Then Tina asked, "You don't think that creepy strangler got her, do you?"

"He's just on the prowl for starlets," I said.

"Then Simone Pearson doesn't exactly qualify," Seymour pointed out.

"Do I?" Tina shuddered and Seymour gave her shoulder a protective squeeze.

"I'll look out for you," he said reassuringly. "None of the victims have been from Empire."

"Does that mean we're due?" She sounded nervous.

"Excuse me, Miss Ferrante, but can you tell me who *this* is?" I held out the publicity photo and pointed to the actress on the left. One look at the photo and she seemed to relax.

"I'd forgotten," Tina said, tapping the picture with a bright-red fingernail and looking at Seymour. "It's a publicity shot from when we were doing that recruitment drive after the Japs bombed Pearl Harbor. The three of us spent about a week standing around flirting with guys in front of the Chinese Theater just up the street. An Army sergeant was with us, and we handed out fliers on how to join up with Uncle Sam."

"I wouldn't be surprised if sometime in the future you get your handprints in the cement over there alongside all those glamorous Hollywood stars," Seymour said. He gave the actress a toothy smile and then munched contentedly on a French fry.

"Who's the dame in the photo?" I asked impatiently.

"Faye Fluellen," Tina said. "Haven't seen *her* for a while. Don't think she's worked much since she got married."

"Can't figure out why she'd wanna get hitched to that crude stuntman," Seymour said. "What's that big ape's name?"

"I don't know," she answered. "I never met him."

"Uh, Wilkins. Yeah, Ted Wilkins. That's his name. Got canned for beating up some extra who came on to his wife when they were all working on the same set. Broke the guy's jaw."

"I heard rumors they're living in a rundown apartment in North Hollywood." Tina was whispering now, and I had to lean close to hear. "They say he bats her around when he gets plastered, but she's afraid to leave him."

Hearing a commotion across the crowded room, we looked up to see the old security guard and two L.A. policemen winding their way around tables as they rapidly headed towards us. A familiar-looking, overweight guy in a baggy suit was with them.

"That's the guy!" The geezer was shouting and pointing in my direction.

"Well, thanks for your cooperation, both of you." I stood up, folded the photograph, and tucked it inside my coat pocket. I hurriedly took out my wallet and removed a business card. "Let me leave this with you, Miss Ferrante, in case you hear from Miss Pearson or think of anything else."

As I snagged my fedora, a flashbulb exploded in our faces. Recoiling from the blinding light, I knocked over my chair and dropped my hat. I attempted a quick getaway but was floored when I tripped over Seymour's outstretched legs, which protruded carelessly from underneath the table. I was helped up almost immediately by the two cops, who roughly clutched my arms and began hauling me away. Another flashbulb went off.

"Don't give us any trouble, bub," one cop said as he tightened his grip. Despite the array of blinking white dots that distorted my vision, when I glanced over my shoulder, I saw fat Bert Brenley, the *Mirror*'s Hollywood reporter. He was replacing the blackened bulb in his camera while he engaged in an animated conversation with Seymour and Tina Ferrante. That damn busybody was always trying to dig up some dirt. I just hoped the actress and her director wouldn't blab every single detail from our conversation.

With every celebrity in the commissary looking our way, we finally reached the exit. The cops released my arms but escorted me to the VISITORS parking area while the old man strutted in front of us. One of the cops tossed me my hat, which he'd undoubtedly recovered from the cafeteria floor. "Can't be a gumshoe without your fedora," he said, chuckling. "But do your peeping somewhere else." I brushed off my hat and stuck it on.

"You wanna press charges?" the other cop asked the geezer as we arrived at my Ford.

"I'll let him off with a warning *this* time."

"It's your call, fella," the same cop said. "We won't even bother writing it up. This joker's already taken up too much of our time."

"The next time you pull a stunt like this, sonny boy, your ass is mine," said the old man, wagging an arthritic finger at me. Both cops laughed loudly as they started walking away.

"I got it under control," the old-timer called after them. "Appreciate your assistance." They got into their nearby squad car and drove off. Luckily for me, the cops were probably in a rush to get back to their lunch break. They were even too lazy to check my ID. And the old man, perhaps in the early stages of senility, must have forgotten to mention my expired investigator's license.

"Hey, pops," I said, "how come that sleazy bastard Brenley just *happened* to be here? What'd you do, tip him off? Is that how you pick up extra money?"

"He's got a press pass. Guess he noticed the cops arrive and just followed 'em. He's just looking for a scoop. That's his job."

"Aren't celebrities afraid he'll entangle them in some cheesy scandal?"

"You know what they say. When you're in showbiz, *any* publicity is better than none at all. Too bad that ain't true for you, peeper. My guess is your employer ain't exactly gonna be overjoyed when he sees your mug in tomorrow's *Mirror*." He laughed.

"What'd your boss say when you told him who I worked for?" I paused at the door of my Ford.

"I never put the call through. With your belligerent attitude, I knew you was nothing but trouble, and I just phoned the cops." As he strolled back to the guard booth, I started up my car and sped towards him. I decided against running him down at the last minute. When I swerved around him, I honked my horn. He jumped like he'd touched a live wire. Driving off the lot, I waved cheerfully at another security guard, who peered quizzically from the booth. In my rearview mirror, I glimpsed the old-timer waving at me, but he was only using his middle finger.

TEN

I took a swallow of coffee, lit another cigarette from the butt I'd been smoking, and snuffed out the stub in the crowded ashtray on my kitchen table. I poured myself another cup and added a healthy dose of brandy. After stopping by the office to check on the mail yesterday, I spent the rest of the afternoon barhopping. I needed a little jolt to deaden my morning hangover.

Then I took another look at the front page of Wednesday's *Mirror*. The huge headline read: CLUELESS DETECTIVE SEARCHES FOR MISSING ACTRESS. A photograph showed the cops accosting me as Howard Seymour and Tina Ferrante looked on in apparent shock. The two had obviously blabbed our entire conversation to Bert Brenley, whose accompanying story revealed that actress Simone Pearson, wife of war hero Vincent McGahee, had been missing for five days. Apparently they'd mentioned my reference to Simone's shoplifting as well as Tina's guess about Muriel's. Brenley had undoubtedly phoned Van Every, pried the unseemly details from the store manager, and then put it all together.

On the day she was supposed to start a new film at Empire Studios, Simone Pearson had a strange encounter with an undercover detective at a swank clothing store and then mysteriously disappeared. Brenley spelled out the incident at Muriel's on Friday. He included an intentionally humorous description of my accusation against Simone, her countercharge, and her temporarily disabling low blow. Brenley never actually accused me of any wrongdoing, but he claimed Van Every had offered the actress a "hundred-dollar bribe" in an attempt to avoid a lawsuit against the store. I doubted Van Every would appreciate Brenley's choice of words. The reporter noted that Simone refused the offer and was last seen angrily departing Muriel's.

In his lurid style, he wondered if the strangler had been waiting for her outside in the storm. Maybe the killer was branching out in his search for victims and was adding "has-been actresses" to his list of starlets. Brenley pointed out that Simone had been fired from Empire in January for "drunken behavior" and hadn't worked in movies since. He suggested that the strangler may have intervened and spoiled her comeback attempt. He even mentioned my puzzling dance number in the pouring rain, speculating that I must've been celebrating Van Every's decision not to call the cops and have me thrown in jail.

Simone's apparently desperate husband had then hired me to locate his missing wife. When reached by phone, McGahee had no comment. Brenley went on to report that yesterday I was forcibly removed from Empire Studios for trespassing, but not until after I had badgered Simone's acquaintances for information about her whereabouts. My disgraceful conduct at both the clothing store and the movie studio, Brenley said, should result in my private investigator's license being revoked. Obviously, he didn't know that it had already expired.

Then Brenley brought up an awkward moment from my past. After years as an investigator for the district attorney's office, I'd been fired by a newly elected D.A., who had run on a platform that included a promise to cut taxpayer expenses by ridding the office of any deadwood. Brenley recommended that I give some serious thought to writing full time for pulp magazines. Private detectives like me were a dime a dozen, according to him, and they should leave real crime investigating to pros such as Nick Drayton, the LAPD detective who'd just been assigned to the Pearson case. Brenley tagged me with a label that would stick: Dime Detective. Drayton told the reporter that the police would pursue all leads in order to find the actress. He then warned that my continued bungling might impede the official police investigation.

As I took a sip of coffee, I unhappily recalled my tenure at the D.A.'s office, where I often interviewed suspects and witnesses in an effort to verify or debunk alibis or to track down leads in criminal cases. Any promising information I unearthed went into a report that was turned over to the police for follow-up. Of course, the cops took all the credit. I'd had numerous run-ins with Drayton over the years. He claimed I wasn't a dogged enough investigator. But I found that the more legwork I did on Drayton's cases, the more time he squandered lounging around his office, nibbling donuts and sipping coffee. To ease my resentment, I started frequenting bars during working hours. His complaints about my job performance most likely contributed to my dismissal from the D.A.'s office. That's when I turned to pulp-fiction writing and, after some early success, decided to open my own detective agency. For Drayton, an ambitious bastard trying to make captain, this high-profile case undoubtedly represented an opportunity to score some promotion points.

After reading the story for a third time, I phoned that libelous SOB Brenley at the *Mirror* to inquire why he hadn't bothered to get my comments on the shoplifting episode.

"What's the use? You'd just deny everything," he said, slamming down the phone. I considered the story nothing but nitpicking on Brenley's part, but a private detective who was roundly ridiculed in the newspaper couldn't expect potential clients to fill his waiting room. Who wanted to hire an investigator whose carelessness resulted in his photo and confidential information about his case splashed on the front page of a sleazy tabloid?

I was starting to adjust to the idea of being back in the ranks of the unemployed when the phone rang. What could it be but more bad news? I resisted as long as I could before finally answering. It was McGahee's butler, Geoffrey, who told me to hold the line for the war hero himself. Another unsatisfied customer, no doubt. First Van Every and now McGahee.

"Mr. Craven, I'm holding a copy of everyone's favorite scandal sheet," McGahee announced.

"I'm considering contacting my attorney and suing Brenley for defamation of character." I was practically shouting into the mouthpiece. "You'll be my first witness since you can testify about your wife's peculiar shopping habits."

"Remember, I'm your client, Mr. Craven. You're still on the case. We're in this together. I want you to know I refused to talk to that despicable reporter when he phoned here. And I'm sending you a hundred-dollar check for all the abuse you took in that tabloid story."

"Aren't the police on the case now?"

"They sure didn't waste any time once they learned of Simone's disappearance. Detective Drayton already paid us a visit. He doesn't approve of your methods. And I'm not crazy about all the publicity you've caused, but perhaps it's best that an official investigation is under way. However, Drayton was interrogating me as if I were a suspect. He was also questioning my sister-in-law Ashley."

"The police usually start a criminal investigation by questioning the victim's next of kin. Mr. McGahee, is your wife's sister at home now?"

"Hold on," he said. I heard some whispering in the background before she got on the line.

"Hello, this is Ashley Greene. How may I help you?" Her voice reminded me of Simone's but without the angry edge.

"This is Sidney Craven. Your brother-in-law hired me."

"Vincent told me about you, Mr. Craven. You know, I've already been quizzed by Detective Drayton."

"I'll be brief, ma'am. Are you married?"

"Divorced," she said. "I kept my ex-husband's name. I thought you wanted to talk about my sister."

"What can you tell me about the last time you saw her?"

"The three of us had been listening to war news on the radio late Thursday. Then at about ten we called it a night. They went to their bedroom, and I went to the guest room down the hall. We just figured Simone left for the studio early in the morning."

"What was her state of mind?" I asked.

"She was tired after spending the whole day at the studio. Simone confided to me that she was worried about restarting her career. My sister's a very fragile person, and the idea of trying to stay sober while making a new movie must have been frightening."

"You think she ran away because of her fear of failure?"

"I think you just put your finger on it, Mr. Craven. Hope I was of some help. One minute. Vincent wants to talk to you again."

"Just a couple more questions, ma'am."

McGahee got back on the line. "Has Drayton contacted you yet, Mr. Craven?"

"No."

"He says he wants to pick your brain. He's curious to find out if you've stumbled onto something that may help the police investigation. Have you?"

"Drayton's a hotshot detective. He doesn't need my help. If you've read the *Mirror* story, you know what I know. I've already talked with one of the starlets in the publicity photo you gave me. I plan on getting in touch with the other one when we hang up." For some reason Brenley hadn't mentioned Faye Fluellen's name in his story. Maybe the two blabbermouths forgot to tell him I was looking for her. They'd told him everything else.

"Call me as soon as you discover any new information," McGahee said.

"Of course."

"I'll get that check out to you ASAP." He hung up.

I wasn't exactly feeling reborn, but I broke the seal on a pint of whiskey anyway. Then, having second thoughts, I recapped the bottle and reached for the phone book.

ELEVEN

"Hello, am I speaking with Miss Faye Fluellen?" I asked. A woman had answered the telephone. As I waited for her response, I heard her breathing softly. I'd found a listing for Ted Wilkins, the ex-stuntman, in the San Fernando Valley phone directory.

"Who's calling, please?" she finally said in a tired voice.

"I'm a detective working on a missing persons case. Are you Miss Fluellen?"

"Mrs. Wilkins. I use my married name now."

"Do you know Simone Pearson?"

There was another pause before she said, "Hey, are you that dopey detective that the *Mirror* says is trying to locate her? Are you that Dime Detective guy?"

"Hell, no, that clown's off the case," I said with a laugh I hoped wasn't too artificial sounding.

"I'd like to help, but I can't talk right now." She abruptly hung up. I underlined her North Hollywood address in the phone book, tore out the page, folded it, and stuffed it in my pants pocket. Then I selected a decent-looking tie and put on my shoulder holster. I checked my .45. I popped out the magazine, then shoved it back into place. The gun hadn't been cleaned lately, but it was loaded. I slipped the Colt into my holster, put on my suit coat, grabbed my hat, and took off. Before driving into the Valley, I stopped at Batson's Coffee House for a late breakfast and another friendly chat with Betty.

Not wanting to sound too anxious, I resisted bringing up Lucy when Betty took my order. As soon as she brought over my waffles, however, I asked nonchalantly, "Did you talk to Lucy?"

"I just got off the phone with her."

"What'd she say?"

"Yesterday, I told her you were just an ordinary private detective, the kind you can find by the dozens in the L.A. phone book. Then today she reads Bert Brenley's front-page story in the *Mirror*."

"Give me a chance to explain," I practically begged.

"Save it, Sid," she said, drifting to another table. I doused my waffles with syrup and took a bite. I pushed away the plate and lit a cigarette.

"That trashy tabloid is fun to read," Betty said, hovering in my vicinity with her coffeepot. "Almost everybody in Bert's stories gets smeared by his insinuations. Readers can choose to believe whatever they want to. Sometimes he just makes stuff up, like the part about you dancing down the sidewalk in the rain. I don't believe it for a minute." She giggled. "Just one look tells me you're not the type of guy who's got any rhythm."

"Glad you can recognize his bunk," I said shamelessly. "What about Lucy?"

"After reading the story, she changed her mind about going out with you."

"Stung by bad timing once again." I was feeling frustrated.

"You don't get it, Sid," Betty said cheerfully. "Now, Lucy *wants* to meet you."

"Huh?"

"Guess she's bored with regular guys. She's looking for someone who's unconventional."

"That's me," I said, laughing.

Ten minutes later Betty brought my check. "Make sure I didn't overcharge you," she said with a smile and moved on. I gave the check a quick look. The total for waffles and coffee was right on the nose. Then I looked again. At the bottom of the check she'd scribbled "Lucy." Then she'd jotted down a phone number. I copied the number onto the back of a business card and plunked down a couple of singles next to my nearly untouched plate.

As I headed for the door, Betty tapped me on the shoulder. "Hope you and Lucy hit it off," she said.

"Why wouldn't we?" I went through the exit and out into the parking lot.

My car started right up for a change. Humming a show tune, I drove down Sunset. I took Cahuenga Pass into the Valley. When I reached North Hollywood, I turned onto Magnolia Boulevard and checked for Faye's street number on the page from my phone book. My old Ford fit in with most of the other cars in the parking lot of the seedy two-story apartment building. I scanned the mail slots in the lobby. The Wilkinses were in apartment number 210. The darkened stairway was littered with cigarette butts and food crumbs. I tried not to flatten too many roaches on my way up. I strolled down the musty-smelling hallway on the second floor and tripped on a rip in the threadbare carpet. Stumbling forward, I regained my balance just in time to come to a wavering stop in front of the right apartment.

I knocked on the door and waited. No response. I knocked louder, much louder.

"Who the hell is it?" a guy yelled from inside the apartment.

"It's your lucky day!" I shouted at the door. "We got a special promotional offer. Today only. Your wife's been randomly selected from hundreds of other housewives." I rambled on nonsensically. "Her name was drawn out of a hat by Mayor Gundy himself. She's the winner of our deluxe vacuum cleaner. Not available in stores. Your wife gets this marvelous machine for free. Guaranteed to perform better than her old vacuum. No strings attached." The door opened just enough to reveal a surly, unshaven Neanderthal in a sweaty tee shirt and striped boxer shorts. He was smoking a poisonous cigar and gripping the neck of a nearly empty beer bottle as he glared down at me.

"We don't want any," he said, slurring his words. "Dangle, take the air, you know, shove off." He tried to slam the door shut, but it smashed into my foot, which I'd unwisely planted in the way.

"It's free," I said with a grimace. "How can a reasonable man like yourself turn down such a fabulous offer?" I was just buying time until I could think of something clever to say. At the moment, however, I was distracted by my throbbing foot.

"So, where *is* this free vacuum cleaner?" He opened the door wider and gazed around the outside hallway. It was a reasonable enough inquiry. While I pondered it, I relocated my foot just in case he decided to slam the door again.

"Vacuum's in my car," I responded. "I got a hernia and can't carry it up the stairs. So, I'll give you my car keys if you'll just walk down to the parking lot. It's a brown two-door Ford. You can get the vacuum out of the trunk while I tell your wife all about it."

"Okay, enough nonsense. What's it you really want? And make it snappy."

"All right, I'll level with you. The vacuums aren't worth a damn. They're just a gimmick to get you to open your door. I'm really taking a survey of housewives in the Valley. We just wanna know how many appliances the little lady owns and how she likes 'em. We pay ten bucks for a five-minute survey."

"You should of said so to begin with. What made you think you could pull a fast one on a guy like me that's been around?" I chose not to answer, but apparently he was too drunk to notice. "You got a questionnaire she fills out or what?" he wondered.

"I got all the questions right up here." I tapped the side of my head with my forefinger.

"Well, give me the ten spot and I'll let you have five minutes to talk with the wife."

"I'll give you five up front and five afterwards."

"Deal," he said as I got out my wallet and handed him a five. "Faye, get me a cold beer and then talk to this guy," he called over his shoulder. To me he said, "You got five minutes, pal, or until I finish my brew, whichever comes first."

He wobbled away, and a peroxide blonde in hair curlers and a bathrobe handed the big goof another bottle and then slouched between the door jamb and the partly opened door. Despite a bruise on the side of her face and a split lip, she was recognizable from the publicity photo.

"I've been listening to your chatter, and you sound like the guy I just talked to on the phone," Faye said in a whisper.

Nodding, I lowered my voice. "What can you tell me about Simone

Pearson?"

After a furtive backwards glance, she said, "Simone called me last week and wondered if I'd like to go with her to an audition at Empire. Guess she was nervous and wanted a friend along to hold her hand. It's the first time I heard from her since…" Faye shook her head and threw up her arms. "Told her my husband won't let me go to the studio anymore. Ted's got a grudge against Hollywood because he got fired for no good reason. He calls it Babylon. Ted thinks movie people are degenerates, and they're a bad influence on somebody like me. He's just trying to protect me. So, I'm officially retired from the movies."

"Look, I don't have much time. Have you talked to Simone since then?"

"Nope. What do you think happened to her? You think it was the strangler?" She was watching me closely.

"That's what I'm trying to find out."

"You know, you look a lot like that private detective in the *Mirror* photo," she said, her voice rising.

"It's an unfortunate resemblance. Look, did Simone have any places she liked to go when she just wanted to get away for a while?"

"Simone liked jazz." Faye lowered her voice. "That girl was bold. She used to go over to the nightclubs on Central, you know, in the mostly colored section. Simone said she was getting lonely and restless, what with her husband overseas and all. She took me once last year when we were both working at the studio—before I got married. She actually got up on stage and did a couple numbers with the dance band. The audience just ate it up. I didn't even know she could sing. And she was real friendly with some Negro musician. Guy played trumpet in the band. His name was Nehemiah…something. He came over and joined us at our table after the set. We were just about the only whites—"

"Hey, what's all the whispering for?" Wilkins suddenly bumped into the door, and it flew all the way open. I glanced into their small living room. A cat was snoozing in a dilapidated easy chair.

"Thank you, Mrs. Wilkins," I said, quickly taking out my wallet. When I shook Faye's hand, I slipped her a folded ten-dollar bill, which she pocketed as she slyly rolled her eyes in the direction of her husband. "You've been very helpful. A detailed analysis of all the data you've given me will definitely help my company."

"By the way, shorty, what company are you with?" Wilkins demanded, belching loudly.

"Great American Gadgets," I replied, handing him his other five. "Be sure to look for GAG products in a store near you. Mention my name and you get a fifty-percent discount. Thanks again." I turned and started down the hallway.

"Hey, you never told me your name," he said.

"It's Saven. Sammy Saven. Easy to remember. It's the name with everybody's favorite four-letter word in it: save. And that's exactly what you do when you buy GAG merchandise." He shouted another question, but I had already rounded the hallway corner and was descending the stairs.

TWELVE

My daydreaming was interrupted by the static hum of the buzzer that was hooked up to my waiting-room door. It was about two, and I was in my office pondering my next move in the Pearson case. Now I had a walk-in customer. I stashed my whiskey bottle in the desk drawer just as my office door swung open. Wearing his customary black suit and pushing back his hat to reveal his receding hairline, Nick Drayton strolled purposefully through my doorway. The detective was about forty and stocky. He had maybe two day's growth of beard on his square chin.

"Good afternoon, detective," I said. "Don't the police knock anymore before entering a private office?"

"Normally we do, but for you I made an exception." He tossed his hat onto one of the two customer chairs in front of my desk, walked over, and extended his hand. I didn't bother getting up. His handshake and accompanying smile were as pleasant as a car wreck. Drayton plopped his flabby ass down in the chair next to the one occupied by his fedora. "I'm here about the Pearson broad. Thought you could be of some help."

I raised my brows in a show of surprise. "You must be a little desperate coming to *me*. How'd you get assigned to the case anyway? Shouldn't it have gone to Hollywood Division? You're with Central."

"Hollywood detectives are working overtime on the Starlet Strangler case. Don't you read the papers? Phones have been ringing day and night over there. So, they've been directing callers elsewhere. We've been handling some of the overflow. All I know is I just happened to take the call when that guy Brenley at the *Mirror* phoned after your fiasco at Empire Studios. He wanted to know if we had any info on the Pearson disappearance. That was the first I heard about it. It pays to be in the right place at the right time."

"Yeah, loafing around the station while the other cops are out tracking down leads," I said.

Drayton flashed a phony smile. "I'll level with you, Sid." He leaned forward as if he was about to share some confidential information with me. "Something about the Pearson case don't smell right, and it's not just your breath." He laughed. "My captain says they're transferring the case to the special unit they got for the strangler. So it's gonna get shuffled in with the damn strangler investigation. I'm running out of time. You got a couple days head start on me. Come on, Sid, throw me a bone for old time's sake." The lazy SOB had expected me to do most of his legwork when I was an investigator for the D.A. I was no longer on the government payroll, but apparently his attitude hadn't changed.

"You told Bert Brenley I was a lousy detective," I said, annoyed. "It was in the paper for everyone to see. Now you want my help?"

"I was misquoted. It happens all the time in that scandal sheet. Talk to me, Sid."

"They're taking away your high-profile case and you want me to cough up some evidence that'll make 'em change their minds. Is that about right?" I was enjoying the moment. I shook a Chesterfield loose from my pack, stuck it in my mouth and got out a wooden match, which I lit on my thumbnail. I put the flame to my cigarette and then—just for laughs—blew smoke rings at Drayton.

"Even you must know the Pearson frail doesn't fit the profile of the dead starlets in the strangler case," he said, fanning away the smoke with his hand. "Her case is more complicated. She's a famous actress who was about to make a new movie. But instead of showing up at the studio to start filming, she gets into a fracas with *you* at a clothing store and then just skips out. Why'd she change her mind about doing the film? I'll bet you it wasn't anything to do with the strangler."

"Females are fickle. Her husband said she's an alcoholic. Drunks are supposed to be unreliable, aren't they?"

"You'd know better than me," he said with a smirk. I let the remark slide. "Maybe she's holed up somewhere with a bottle," he guessed. "Or maybe her husband did her in."

"And his motive?" I asked. "Did you forget he's a paralyzed war hero with missing toes?"

"Piss on his toes. The *real* heroes are the ground forces. They're the ones who stormed the damn beaches on D-Day a couple weeks ago. And lost their lives. Vincent McGahee was a flyboy—with a millionaire father—who got his plane shot down. Lost some toes. So what. He gets a ticket back home to his mansion, but the fighting goes on."

"It's just awful. Some guys have all the luck."

"Maybe she was snatched," he suggested. "Everyone knows the old man's got a fortune."

"Guess the kidnappers forgot to send a ransom note."

Drayton glared at me. "You were one of the last people to see Simone Pearson in town."

"That's right—along with dozens of shoppers."

"According to witnesses I've questioned, she did quite a number on you at Muriel's. She left the store on Friday afternoon shortly before you danced your way down the sidewalk. Too bad I missed your little show. I like a good laugh. But let's get serious for a minute. Can you account for your whereabouts for the rest of the afternoon?"

"I'm not even gonna answer that question."

"Look, Craven, I'm just doing my job. You gotta admit you had the motive. I mean the way that bitch kicked your ass after you tried to molest her. Who could blame you for wanting revenge? That *Mirror* reporter certainly got all the salacious details. Did you follow Simone in your car and try to finish what you started with her in the store? Did things get out of hand? What'd you do to her? You didn't kill her, did you?"

"A jury would howl at such a scenario, but it might make a decent plot for a crime story." I was getting aggravated. "If you believe the crap they print in that tabloid, then you should have your head examined."

"Who knows what's true and what's not?" he sneered.

"You're full of shit, Drayton, and we both know it." I angrily jabbed out my cigarette in the ashtray on my desk. "Instead of harassing *me*, you should—"

"All right, Sidney, don't have a heart attack. Can't you tell when you're being kidded? You know, that *Mirror* story could of been a severe blow to your reputation—if you had one." Throwing his head back, he loosed a loud horselaugh. I gritted my teeth and waited. "Tell me what you got, Sid."

"You just told me Brenley had all the details in his story. Why don't you read it again? This time use a dictionary and take some notes."

"I could haul you downtown for withholding evidence and hold you overnight in jail."

"What evidence? What's the crime? People go missing all the time. If you got off your lazy butt and did some snooping, maybe you could find who's really to blame for Simone's disappearance. You crack this case and you probably got your promotion. But now it looks like it's gonna be taken out of your hands unless you come up with a telltale lipstick smudge or maybe an incriminating fingerprint." It was my turn to laugh.

"Later, Dime Detective." He seized his hat and made a quick exit.

I wondered about Drayton's comment on how the police were handling the Pearson case. I called Larry Elam, an old friend from the D.A.'s office. We had both worked as investigators. About the time I'd been fired, he had been promoted to a desk job.

"Just been reading about your adventures in the *Mirror*," he said. "You never got publicity like that when you worked here, Sid. Now that you're famous, I can tell everybody I knew you way back when." He laughed.

"Glad you're enjoying yourself, Larry. Let's talk shop for a minute. What can you tell me about the Pearson case?"

"Let's see." He rustled some papers. "Can't find the file, but I know your buddy Drayton has the case for now. According to office scuttlebutt, it's being reassigned to the strangler detail."

"But why? It doesn't belong there. It'll get lost in the shuffle."

"That's the idea." He lowered his voice. "You know who Simone Pearson's father-in-law is?"

"Victor McGahee."

"Bingo! While you chew that one over, Sid, I got a load of daily detective reports to review."

"One more minute, Larry. When I worked for the D.A., I heard all sorts of nasty rumors about old man McGahee. You know what I'm talking about."

"Yeah. He's been accused of fraudulent banking practices and income tax evasion—just to name two. But nothing ever sticks. He's got smart accountants. They're always two steps ahead of the law."

"He's got connections," I said.

"You're right. He's always handing out donations to worthy causes and making campaign contributions."

"More like bribes."

"Call 'em what you want. We can't touch the old man."

"Didn't he have problems when he was in Houston?"

"Uh-huh," Elam said, making a yawning sound. "When McGahee was in the oil business, his silent partners accused him of bilking them out of their fair share of the profits. They sued the old man but then settled out of court. And he sold his share of the company to his former partners just before the Depression hit. The man's got uncanny timing." Elam chuckled. "When the economy started to improve, McGahee went into investment banking and made a name for himself by earning big bucks for his clients in the stock market. Then came the rumors of dubious investment schemes. Maybe spread by some unhappy customers or by other brokers who didn't have McGahee's success. Anyway, when Texas authorities started looking into the old man's banking business, he packed up and moved his company here. They never found enough evidence to bring charges. Now he's helping the rich get richer in L.A., and he's good friends with Mayor Gundy. You'd have to fight city hall if you want to bring McGahee down."

"I'm just trying to solve a missing persons case," I said with a laugh. "But now I know what I'm up against."

"Try not to step on McGahee's toes." He hung up.

THIRTEEN

"I'm a riveter on an assembly line," Lucy said. "I *knew* you'd never get it."

"That was gonna be my next guess," I said, laughing. We were talking on the phone.

"After my divorce I had to find a reliable job," she explained. "Can't beat working for Uncle Sam."

"I used to have a government job. I was an investigator in the D.A.'s office."

"Yeah, but you got canned, Sidney," Lucy pointed out. "Don't worry, I won't hold it against you."

I had called her shortly after my talk with Larry Elam. Like her sister-in-law Betty, she could really bend your ear. Since she already knew my line of work, she'd wanted me to guess hers.

"After reading Bert Brenley's story in the *Mirror*," she said, "I feel like I already know you."

"Just for the record, I didn't lay a hand on Simone Pearson." I was tired of sounding defensive. "Who you gonna believe? Look at the Pearson dame—apparently quitting her job and then just disappearing. She's a little loony."

"And you're not? Dancing in the rain outside Muriel's and sneaking onto that movie lot." She laughed.

"Sometimes you have to improvise when you find yourself in sticky situations," I said casually.

"You could probably say the same thing about her."

"Whose side are you on, Lucy?"

"It's a close call, but I'm taking your side, Sid. You gotta tell me what Simone Pearson filched."

"Two bras and a pair of nylons. Just stuck 'em in her pockets." I recounted the episode from my point of view.

"To think she beat you up and then framed *you* for assaulting *her*," Lucy said almost admiringly.

"It was a diversionary tactic to avoid getting arrested."

"And it worked. She's good."

"How about a boat ride to Catalina Island on Saturday?" I was ready to change the topic. "You get weekends off?"

"My weekends are free but ixnay on the riptay, Sidney. Guess you didn't hear about it. They closed the island to tourists. The military's been using it for special training."

"How about a night at the movies? You can choose from whatever's playing."

"Just checked my clock. Gotta run, Sid. I'm on the afternoon shift at the plant. My ride will be here any minute. We gotta be there by four."

"You work till midnight?"

"Weekdays only. I'll check the paper to see what's playing. Call me." She hung up.

I reached for a cigarette, but my pack was empty. I left the office and went down the hallway towards Wanda's. I was in a good mood for a change. Things were looking up: a hundred-dollar check on the way, and a weekend date.

"How's business, Candy?" I asked the sexy young secretary when I opened Wanda's door.

"We'd be doing better if you made a purchase once in a while," she said, loudly snapping her gum. "Boss is in the back counting the money." Candy wore too much perfume and too much makeup, but she was usually good for a laugh. She resumed her typing, and I wandered through the open door and into Wanda's office.

"What d'you know, Sidney?" Wanda asked. She was sorting through a stack of order forms on her desk. Dozens of boxes were stacked against the walls. Mannequin heads, topped by a variety of wigs, were arranged on shelves adjacent to the doorway. Although she welcomed walk-in customers, Wanda ran a mail-order business. Her splashy catalogue featured wigs, toupees, and hats. Customers who didn't know their size could come in for a fitting.

"I need a nicotine fix."

"You've come to the right place," Wanda said, leaning back in her creaking chair. "Help yourself." Wanda looked comfortable in her brown and white frock. She was a friendly neighbor, single, about forty, and about three hundred pounds. I grabbed her pack of Lucky Strikes, which was resting next to an ashtray overflowing with half-smoked cigarettes. I shook out two Luckies, stuck both in my mouth, and lit them with a match I struck on the sole of my shoe. I'd seen it done in a movie but had never tried it—until now.

"What you gonna do for an encore?" She laughed as I handed her one of the smokes.

"Disappear," I said. "Wish I could stick around and shoot the breeze, but I'm on a big case."

"I read all about it in the *Mirror*. You're practically a celebrity." She winked. "Now's the time for a brand-new fedora. We got all the latest styles."

"I'll take a rain check," I said over my shoulder. I waved to Candy as I passed her desk. She glanced up and nodded without missing a beat on her typewriter. Maybe seeing Candy at her typewriter inspired me. Back in my office, I felt the urge to work on some detective fiction. I sat down at my desk and began typing. Ideas came to me in a rush. Sometimes it was like that. I'd get lost in my own story. When I glanced at the wall clock, it was eight. I grabbed the phone book and made a number of calls. Then I grabbed my hat and headed for the door.

FOURTEEN

The applause began before the final trumpet note faded away. As Nehemiah Wright and His Sweet Delights soaked up the audience adulation, each band member—the piano player, bass player, drummer, and trumpeter— took a short bow. Then the Sweet Delights, two colored girls in skintight, low-cut dresses, waved to the raucous nightclub crowd. The set over, band members and singers left the small stage for their break. The couples on the dance floor reluctantly dispersed.

The trumpet player, however, lingered as he opened a folded scrap of paper he'd just been handed. The waiter who had delivered the note then pointed a finger at a corner table where I sat alone. Nehemiah Wright followed the finger with his eyes, shook his head slowly, and turned his back on me. He took a second look at the note on which I had scribbled just one word: "Simone."

Before leaving my office, I had spent about half an hour paging through the telephone directory and calling nightclubs in South Central L.A. Negroes had been flocking to the area as factory jobs became available after the start of the war. It had become a center for colored merchants, social organizations, and jazz clubs. On each call, I had asked the same question: "Ever hear of a trumpet player named Nehemiah?" I finally traced him to a dive called the Red-Hot Charcoal in a mixed block on Central Avenue. And now he was heading my way.

"Have a seat, Mr. Wright," I said as he pulled out a chair and joined me. About forty, he was tall, thin and dapper in his pin-striped tuxedo. "I'm

Ralph Maven, a talent scout, and I'm looking for your girlfriend," I abruptly announced. "I've found the perfect film part for her Hollywood comeback. The problem is I can't find her."

"Who are you kidding, Mr. Craven?" he demanded.

"It's Maven," I insisted, "and I was hoping you could help me locate Simone Pearson."

"Look, Mr. Dime Detective, I recognize your face from the photo they ran in this morning's *Mirror*, and I never forget a name. I don't believe everything I read in that scandal sheet, but there's no doubt it's you in that picture. For your information, Miss Pearson was never my girlfriend."

"You may be surprised to hear that I've got an eyewitness who's seen you two together and says otherwise."

"Look," he said, annoyed. "Simone stopped by the club for a short visit a week ago. Told me she was back from an audition at her movie studio and got the part. She was excited about starting a new movie. That's the first time I saw her since I can't remember when. It's been weeks. When it comes to Simone, I lose track of time."

"How'd you two meet?"

"She used to hang out at some of the jazz joints on Central." Nehemiah leaned back in his chair and glanced around the club. Tables surrounded the dance floor, and a bar curved off to the side. I didn't notice many empty seats. A small but noisy group had convened at a craps table against one wall.

"Simone said the Charcoal was her favorite spot," he continued. "She got up on stage and joined the band maybe twice a week. She was good for business. I tried to talk her into becoming a regular, but she had her movie career. Some of our customers were probably attracted by the oddity of a white gal crooning torch songs at the Charcoal. Whenever people brought it up, Simone would just tell 'em she was a mulatto. She didn't want no trouble. But I don't think anybody really gave a damn about her skin color once they heard her rendition of a familiar song. She had a bluesy style that had 'em coming back for more. If she didn't know all the words, she'd just scat her way around the music, half a beat behind. Reminded me of Billie Holiday. That's how good she was."

"Guess you discovered her secret talent. I don't think her movie fans knew about it."

"And the crowd here didn't know she was a Hollywood celebrity," he said. "Simone told me she auditioned for a part in a Hollywood musical once, but the director said her singing wasn't sweet enough, and he even ridiculed her voice. Naturally, she got shy about performing. White audiences just couldn't appreciate her offbeat style. If you closed your eyes when she was on stage, you'd swear a colored gal was nailing them notes."

"Sounds like you were Simone's biggest fan."

"She was such a hit, I added two girl singers to my band." He shook his head. "I don't know how I ever did without 'em. Now the place is hopping every night. If Simone ever made up her mind to come back, I'd have myself a trio of Delights." He smiled fondly at the idea.

"She just stopped showing up?"

"That's right, until her visit last week. That's all I can tell you."

"Sure you're not holding anything back? For instance, were you in love with her?"

"We had a business relationship, Mr. Craven," he said bluntly. "Now, you'll have to excuse me. I gotta make some music." He strolled back to the bandstand, where the other musicians were already tuning up.

I thought about what little progress I had made on the case. Then I decided not to think about it. The night was still young, and I had some pocket money: a twenty plus some singles. As the band kicked off its next set, I held up my empty glass and signaled for a waiter to bring me another whiskey.

FIFTEEN

On the last number of the band's set, Nehemiah stepped forward for a jazzy trumpet solo. Just as I caught his chilly gaze, he blew a high note that felt like a poisoned dart aimed at one of my vital parts. With only a handful of whites in the joint, I was already a touch uncomfortable and decided to hit the road after downing my third whiskey and soda.

Then a giant black man wearing a green suit, a yellow bow tie, blue brogues, and clutching a purple derby in his fist seated himself at my table. He had been standing in front of the nightclub when I drove up earlier. Only a blind man wouldn't have noticed him. He had eyed me as I got out of my car and walked towards the club. "This is a colored joint," he said, blocking the door. I told him I was here to see Mr. Wright on business. He'd thought about it for a minute. Then he made a hawking sound, leaned over and spit on the pavement.

"That doesn't look right," I said, glancing down at the wad of snot between my shoes. "You might want to consult a doctor." He scowled but stepped aside, and I swung open the door to the club.

Now the guy was sitting next to me. "I'm Stanley, a friend of the bandleader," he said gruffly. "Mr. Wright wants to talk to you in private. And he don't want you running off at the mouth to nobody about his business. It's my job to make sure everything stays hush-hush. Get my meaning?"

I nodded. With his loud voice and gaudy attire, Stanley didn't seem particularly well suited for the task. But he wasn't the only flamboyant character in the noisy nightspot. The players in the band and the couples on the dance floor weren't exactly dressed like wallflowers.

"What's the deal?" I asked.

"There's an alleyway next to the club. I'll see you there in ten minutes." He stood up and sauntered away. I took a couple of puffs, killed my cigarette, and gulped down the rest of my drink. Then I pushed my way through the crowd towards the door. The bandstand was empty now. I tipped the hatcheck girl when she retrieved my fedora. Once outside, I looked down the street. My car was parked in the shadows under a burned-out streetlight—just where I'd left it. In this neighborhood that was a good sign.

I heard a piercing whistle and turned to see Stanley standing at the edge of the dark alleyway alongside the Charcoal. I casually wandered over. An auto repair garage was on the other side of the alley. The sign out front said: Jerome's Auto Body and Painting. I foolishly followed Stanley into the shadows.

"Can I see some identification?" he asked. When I reached into my suit coat for my wallet, Stanley plunged his fist into the pit of my stomach. As I bent over in pain, my forehead collided with his rising knee. Jerked upright again, I was knocked out with a vicious right hook to the jaw.

I woke up flat on my back and in complete darkness. A couple of sniffs told me I was surrounded by garbage. Feeling around, I touched empty bottles and cans and most likely coffee grounds and orange peels. I quickly withdrew my hand after a small creature—undoubtedly a rat—tried to run up my arm. When I started to get up, I banged my head against something solid and tumbled back down. Despite feeling dizzy, I was driven by the sound of scampering rodents to make another try. Scrambling around and pushing with my shoulder, I was able to dislodge a large piece of plywood, which had been blocking my movements, and get to my feet. I was standing in the bed of an old pickup truck that was parked in the alley between the nightclub and the body shop. I was halfway up to my knees in an assortment of trash.

The dismal scene was dimly lit by a nearby streetlight. Tires, rusted bumpers and fenders, and other old car parts were piled along the sides of the two buildings. There was enough scrap metal for a couple of Sherman tanks. I pushed the heavy plywood lid over the side of the junkyard truck and jumped down. That vehicle wasn't going anywhere anytime soon. It had four flat tires. I had a splitting headache and a swollen jaw. I took a quick inventory of my teeth—two were loose—but they were all in place. A sour-smelling residue was clinging to my clothes, and I made a mental note to drop off my suit at the dry cleaners if I survived the night.

When I peered into the street from the edge of the alley, I noticed my car was missing. Not a good sign. A cursory search of my pockets revealed that my keys, gun and money were also gone. I still had my empty wallet. A car came slowly up the street and parked right across from the nightclub. It was a Ford—not unlike mine. In fact, it *was* mine. Stanley, jingling the car keys, and another man got out and went towards the Charcoal. They both were about the same age, probably middle thirties. The other man, who was short and heavyset, was rubbing his lower spine.

"I think I threw out my back helping you heft that damn white boy," he said. "I'm gonna be in a world of hurt tomorrow. I probably won't be able to get outta bed."

"Jerome, my man, I think you invented bitching," Stanley said, laughing as he patted him on the shoulder. "After I use the toilet, we'll take care of business." They exchanged greetings with a handful of men who were now loitering in front of the nightclub. Then they disappeared inside. Above the door was a bright-orange neon sign: RED-HOT JAZZ. Flickering on and off, it beckoned passersby to join the good times inside. I'd already had my quota of good times for tonight.

I backtracked into the alley and attempted to come up with a plan to retrieve my stolen property. A weapon of some kind would come in handy. I tripped and went down on all fours. When I looked around, I discovered a recklessly placed wooden pallet. A number of its slats were missing and one was wobbly. Despite an aggravating struggle, I couldn't wrench the loose slat from the pallet. Then I noticed a whole stack of pallets just a couple feet away. Next to them was a stockpile of slats. Maybe someone—wanting wood to build something on the cheap—had been dismantling pallets with a pry bar. It was okay with me. I went over and selected a slat that was stout enough to make a good weapon and brandished it like a baseball bat.

In the darkness at the alley's edge, I watched a mixed couple—a black man and a white girl—enter the Red-Hot Charcoal. With the wooden slat resting on my shoulder, I waited. In about ten minutes, the door to the nightclub swung open. Stanley and his friend stepped out and strode down the sidewalk towards the alley. I quickly retreated into the darkness, taking refuge behind the rusty truck. Peeking from the shadows, I picked up their conversation as they approached.

"Listen, Stanley, that heap ain't worth more than thirty bucks, and you know it." They both stopped and faced each other.

"I know what I know, Jerome, my man, and I know I ain't taking less than fifty for that vehicle. You seen for yourself how smooth that baby rides."

"Must of been the road that was rough." Jerome laughed. "Come on, Stanley. Be reasonable."

"Like I told you before, give it a quick paint job and nobody's gonna recognize the motherfucker. Just another hot car you can unload for a goodly profit."

"Take forty and you got yourself a deal." Jerome extended a handful of bills towards my assailant.

"You're a cheap son of a bitch." Stanley took the cash and tossed Jerome the keys. "You just bought yourself some wheels." The two men shook, and Stanley began counting the money.

"What you gonna do with white boy?" Jerome aimed a thumb at the old pickup.

"I don't know. I was thinking I might climb in there and piss on him."

Jerome burst out laughing as he walked away. "Later, man."

Stanley started over with his count. When Jerome disappeared around the corner of the alley, I stepped from my hiding place and crept forward. Stanley heard my footsteps and started to turn just as I swung my wooden club at the back of his head. He said, "Hey, man..." But apparently he lost his train of thought when the blow landed with a solid crack. Looking befuddled, he slowly brought his arms up to protect himself. Too slowly.

I wound up and gave him another whack on the head. His purple hat fell off and the hunk of wood split in half, but the impact stunned him. The bills slipped from his fingers and fluttered to the ground. Hands hanging helplessly at his sides, Stanley began staggering around in a daze. I discarded my fractured weapon and searched him. Somehow managing to stay on his feet, he offered no resistance. I grabbed my .45 from his coat pocket and returned it to my shoulder holster. I filched his wallet from his pants pocket and stepped aside just before he dropped to his knees and toppled over sideways onto the concrete alleyway.

I took a bunch of bills from his wallet and then scooped up the money he had dropped. He began groaning and then rolled onto his back. I tossed his wallet on top of him. In the dim light I counted the money, about one hundred and twenty dollars. I'd got my original pocket money back plus a hefty bonus, which more than made up for my missing fedora—apparently knocked off and lost when Stanley attacked me.

Rushing towards the alleyway entrance, I arrived just in time to see Jerome helping one of the Sweet Delights into my Ford and closing the passenger door. While he strutted back around the car, I ran into the street after him. He squeezed his bulky body under the wheel and shut the door. Out of breath, I approached the driver's side as he started the car and rolled down the window.

"Hey, Jerome," I said, "I'll give you fifty bucks for my old wheels."

"What you talking about, man?" he said with a look of genuine puzzlement, followed by a sly grin. "Don't tell me Stanley just let you go. Where the hell is he?" Jerome glanced around. The same loafers were hanging out by the club's entrance, but the dark alley looked empty.

I quickly counted out fifty dollars from my wallet and waved the money in his face. "Come on, you paid forty bucks for this Ford. You can make a ten-dollar profit."

He snatched the fistful of bills from my grip. "I'll take the money *and* the car, chump. Now scram." He turned to the Sweet Delight. "What say we get the show on the road, Loretta, honey?" Jerome stuffed the cash into the pocket of his suit coat and put the car in gear. I reached in and turned off the motor.

"Hey, white boy, I'm gonna put a hurting on you." His anger quickly turned to surprise when I pulled out my .45 and jabbed it in his face. Loretta screamed. She opened her door and jumped out. Running around the car towards the club, she broke one of her heels and limped across the street. The commotion had roused the guys standing by the Charcoal's entrance.

"Get out, Jerome!" I jerked open his door. He was sweating as he climbed out of the car.

Then he raised his arms over his head and started yelling. "Don't shoot, you crazy bastard! If you want this piece of shit that bad, just take it!" As Jerome backed into the middle of the street, Loretta was waving her broken shoe at me and talking excitedly to the idlers in front of the club. They casually started moving in my direction. I got into the car and slammed the door. I put my gun next to me on the seat.

"What's the problem, Jerome?" one of them shouted.

"Man's crazy!" he responded.

Then Stanley, holding a hand to his bloody head, staggered from the alleyway. "Don't let that white boy get away!" he hollered. When I tried to crank the engine, it hesitated but then rumbled to life. A couple of the loafers finally showed some urgency and hurried across the street. As I lurched away from the curb, I heard a loud bang and ducked my head. But it was only the passenger door swinging shut. One guy smacked his fist on the trunk of the car, but I was soon tearing down Central.

When I stopped at a red light in the next block, my heart was racing, and my hands were trembling on the wheel. I noticed that my apartment and office keys were still on my key ring. I looked in my rearview mirror. No cars were behind me. On the way over from my office, I had the feeling I was being followed by a red Lincoln Continental. But just before I got to the Charcoal, the car had turned down another street. Needing a drink to settle my jangled nerves, I headed for the nearest liquor store.

SIXTEEN

My two favorite L.A. papers ran accounts of Simone Pearson's tragic death on their front pages Thursday morning, along with the same grainy photo of the actress. Returning from the corner newsstand, I'd spread out both papers on my kitchen table. While I sipped a cold cup of coffee, I took a look at the *Mirror*. Wednesday afternoon, Ashley Greene, summoned to the county morgue by the police, had made a positive ID of her sister's body. The name on the toe tag used to identify the corpse was then changed from Jane Doe to Simone Pearson, the *Mirror* reported.

Not in the mood for the tabloid's tawdry style, I turned to the *Times* for a more straightforward chronology of Simone's death and the subsequent discovery and identification of her body. The LAPD had received a phone tip on Monday afternoon. A caller claimed to have seen sunlight reflecting off a wrecked car in a canyon below a desolate mountain road not far from the ocean. Arriving on the scene, fire department rescue workers descended the steep canyon side, still slippery from the weekend's heavy rainfall. Near a crashed vehicle, they retrieved the body of a female, who had been in her middle thirties. Evidently the woman's car had veered off the road and plunged into the valley below. Authorities speculated that the driver's door had popped open during the car's turbulent descent and the driver was flung out.

The woman, her neck broken and skull smashed, had no identification on her. After apparently bursting into flames during the crash, the car, now a mangled web of twisted and blackened steel, offered no clues. The cops recovered a scorched license plate from the vehicle, but it was unreadable.

The corpse was taken to the morgue and classified as Jane Doe. Unable to be more precise because of the body's condition, the coroner put the time of death at "some point between Thursday night and Friday afternoon." When police later learned about the disappearance of Simone Pearson, someone in the department put two and two together. While Simone's invalid husband, Vincent McGahee, remained in his mansion, her sister identified the corpse.

The official coroner's report indicated that the victim, after consuming enough alcoholic drinks to become intoxicated, had been involved in a fatal car crash on a hazardous roadway. While the death appeared to be accidental, the coroner didn't rule out suicide. He went on to say there was no indication of foul play.

On Friday, presumably the last day of her life, according to the *Times*, the actress had skipped the first day of shooting on a new movie and then inexplicably showed up at Muriel's. While at the clothing store, Simone had an altercation with a private detective who accused her of shoplifting. The detective couldn't be reached for comment. The reporter, Ben Luper, had probably tried to phone me about the same time I was getting roughed up and robbed outside the Charcoal.

Although there was some confusion about what actually happened during the scuffle at the store, witnesses agreed Simone was extremely distressed when she departed that afternoon. A few hours later, while intoxicated, she evidently drove to her death off a lonely canyon road. When asked, the coroner agreed that such a scenario was entirely plausible. Simone's husband told the *Times* she had a history of shoplifting and binge drinking, but he emphatically denied she had ever been suicidal. With numerous comments from Drayton and Van Every, much of the story was a rehash of the *Mirror*'s report yesterday.

My search was over. I pushed away the paper and stared idly out the window. I had been trying to locate a woman whose body had been in a drawer in the county morgue. Rummaging through my stack of recent newspapers, I found Tuesday's *Times*. There was plenty of war and strangler coverage. I finally spotted an item on one of the inside pages. It said the body of an unidentified auto-wreck victim had been recovered from the bottom of a canyon near the ocean on Monday.

No longer unknown, Simone had made the front page today. Although I'd met her only once and was the target of her unwarranted hostility, I felt an odd sense of loss. One less person was walking around in the world. And I may have somehow played a part in her undoing. Wincing from the recollection of my encounter with her, I looked at my watch. It was 10 A.M. Even if I stopped at Batson's, I could still get to my office before noon.

Maybe somebody would be looking for a detective. Maybe somebody would call with a job offer. Maybe McGahee's check would be in the mail. I found a spare gray hat on the shelf in the back of my closet. I changed from my tee shirt and casual trousers into an unwrinkled dress shirt and my standby suit. Then I picked out a colorful tie in an attempt to brighten my mood.

Betty held up two fingers to make a victory sign when I strolled into Batson's. "You were a hit with Lucy on the phone." Then she shook her head. "But now you're out of work. The paper said they found your missing actress."

"Just a bump in the road," I said, trying to smile.

"That's the attitude, Sid." She filled my coffee cup. "Something will come up sooner or later."

"Just coffee, Betty. I gotta get to the office and check my mail."

"Maybe you got a client in your waiting room right now."

When I got off the elevator at the tenth floor of the Chandler Building and walked to my office, I half-expected to find a client relaxing on my couch while flipping through an old magazine. But my waiting room was as empty as a flat tire. And nothing in the mail but advertisements and another warning about my overdue office rent. This notice was in even larger print than the previous one, and my landlord had tacked on a ten-dollar late fee. I took some comfort in recalling that my apartment rent was paid up.

As I took out the office bottle and sat back in my swivel chair, the phone rang. It was McGahee's butler. "My employer no longer requires your services," he said.

"Don't tell me he expects a refund."

"He's instructed me to inform you that you may keep his generous retainer, although your performance was unsatisfactory."

"What about the additional payment he promised?" I sounded a little anxious.

"Really, Mr. Craven. You can't be serious," he said, snickering.

"Why not? I've been roughed up and slandered. My car was stolen. So was my gun. I even lost my hat."

"And you think you're entitled to another check? That would be like giving your dog a bone for chewing up your newspaper." He snorted.

"Hey, Geoffrey, tell your boss he can take his check and ram it up your—"

He slammed down the receiver. The phone rang again. It was my literary agent, Morrie Provost. "You're hot now, Sidney," he said excitedly. "Your name's been in the newspapers two days in a row. The wire services picked up the story, and it's been running in papers all around the country. It doesn't matter that the missing celebrity you've been searching for was already dead. Or that she beat you up before she vanished. It's not exactly the sort of publicity we want. But it's publicity all the same. Listen, I just got off the phone with an editor at one of the pulp magazines. We could get top dollar, Sid. Please, say you've got some detective fiction ready for me." Pressure like that wouldn't put a dent in my writer's block.

"Got a bad connection, Morrie," I said. "Can't hear a word you're saying. Call you back later." I hung up and took a swig of whiskey. I wasn't in the mood for Morrie, but he had a point. All the newspaper publicity was a good break for a writer; however, it was the kiss of death for a detective. I might as well take my name out of the phone book.

I tried to expel Simone's sad story from my mind. Maybe I could come up with a decent crime story after all. I'd been on a roll yesterday, definitely chipping away at my writer's block. I took out the pages I had written and skimmed them. Something was wrong. Some joker must've sneaked into my office and replaced my excellent prose with this crap. The building's security was becoming slack. I took another swig from my bottle and shook a cigarette from my pack.

The phone rang. My old friend Wesley Renfro was on the line. He was a freelance insurance investigator, and he was calling about Simone Pearson. Renfro said he was working for Uptowner Life, the company that provided insurance for Empire Studios.

"The Pearson dame didn't even show up for her new movie," I noted. "How could she be covered by Uptowner?"

"She signed a deal with Empire to make that movie," he said. "She was insured at the time of her death. It's a standard policy. And Uptowner's liable for a thirty-grand payout to the beneficiary."

"Let me guess. Vincent McGahee."

"Bull's eye!"

"That SOB just stiffed me for one hundred dollars. And now he's gonna get—"

"He won't see a dime of it if I can show that his wife wrecked her car on purpose."

"How you gonna do that?"

"With your help, Sid," he said, chuckling. "The woman was an alcoholic. She was unhinged. She walked out on her movie. And she assaulted you when you caught her shoplifting."

"It's heartening to know you believe *my* version of what happened." I laughed. "Not everybody does."

"Of course I believe your version. It fits my suicide narrative. She was a troubled woman. What's your snooping unearthed about her past?"

"Nothing that really points to suicide. If she was gonna take her own life, wouldn't she have done it the easy way? You know, with sleeping pills."

"No, Sid. You gotta think positive. Do some more digging. We need a professional opinion on her mental condition. I'll pay your daily rate. Still twenty?"

"Twenty-five plus expenses."

"Guess you gave yourself a raise after you became a celebrity." He snorted. "It's okay with me. By the way, Dime Detective, I like your new handle. Hope you can live up to it." He laughed. "Look, I'm tied up with a couple other cases. You've got some promising leads, right?"

"Of course," I said. I just couldn't think of any at the moment.

"I'll be in touch." He hung up.

Suddenly, I felt tired. I was still recovering from my night on the town. Even counting my respite in the rusty truck, I didn't get much sleep last night. My headache had returned, and now my back was bothering me. I went into my waiting room and stretched out on the couch. It was finally getting some use.

SEVENTEEN

Before the first shovelful of dirt was tossed into the open grave, I turned and walked back towards my car. Not a part of the funeral procession, I had parked on the street outside the cemetery. At the gravesite, the priest had voiced the usual solemn clichés as rain slanted down. Two dozen mourners had formed a ragged horseshoe around Simone Pearson's grave. After attending the private service at Herkimer's Mortuary in downtown L.A., they had accompanied the hearse to the cemetery in West Hollywood.

Simone's obituary, including a summary of her short career, had appeared in Friday's *Times*. I'd read it twice this morning, over coffee and cigarettes, as the sky got darker outside my apartment window. On a local radio station, playing in the background, the weatherman was calling for rain. I had taken yet another look at the article.

Born in San Francisco some thirty-five years ago, Simone had attended U.C. Berkeley, where she studied acting, but dropped out of college after her second year and moved to Hollywood to pursue a career in films. After countless auditions, Simone was signed as a contract player by Empire Studios. For her first two years she played mostly bit parts. Then she was cast as the scatterbrained sidekick of the female lead in a screwball comedy and got rave reviews. In the following years, she demonstrated her flair for comedy in a series of supporting roles in major Empire productions. She also starred in numerous B movies for the studio. I had seen two of the handful of films listed in the paper.

At the premiere of *Life Is Just a Gamble*, one of her biggest hits, Simone met Vincent McGahee. Six months later they were married. The following day, the Japanese bombed Pearl Harbor, and Vincent enlisted in the Army Air Corps. After only a short time together, the newlyweds were split apart for the next two and a half years until Vincent's recent return as a wounded war hero reunited them. Then last week Simone was killed in a tragic car crash.

She was survived by her husband, heir to the McGahee oil fortune, and her sister, Ashley Greene. The last line of the obit named the funeral home, where Simone's body—no longer in a drawer in the morgue—was awaiting burial this afternoon in a private ceremony.

I had grabbed the phone and called the mortuary. When I asked for the time of Simone Pearson's burial ceremony and the name of the cemetery, I was put on hold. The funeral director got on the line, and I repeated my request.

"That information isn't available to the general public," he replied firmly.

"I'm Buddy Graven, Simone's uncle. I just flew in from out of town, and I'm at the airport."

"You'll have to check with Vincent McGahee. He's expected here shortly."

"He's not answering his phone," I said.

"He's probably on his way as we speak. Why don't you meet him and the rest of the family right here? After the funeral service, Mr. Graven, you can join the procession to the cemetery."

"I only have time for the burial," I said, trying to sound rushed. "I'm a busy man. I've got a hundred and one things to do. And not enough time. I've got to catch a flight back to New York in a few hours. There's just no way—"

"For heaven's sake, relax," he said. "You could have a heart attack. It might be *your* funeral if you don't calm down." He chuckled softly.

"Look, I'm in the business myself," I said with a sigh. "I'm a wholesaler. We handle everything from caskets to gravestones. We got a special this month on embalming fluid." I paused while he thought that one over.

"Would I have to purchase in quantity?" he finally asked.

"Hell, no." When I got off the phone, I had what I was looking for.

I'd arrived early. Sitting in my car, I killed time daydreaming about my upcoming date with Lucy. I was on my third cigarette when the procession of cars began entering the cemetery. I turned up my coat collar and bent down the brim of my gray fedora in order to ward off the steady drizzle as I approached the gravesite. Hidden by a cluster of palm trees, I managed to stay out of view. With the binoculars I normally used to follow the horses around the track at Hollywood Park, I focused on the group of mourners. Standing next to Vincent, who was in his wheelchair, Ashley had her hand on his shoulder. I assumed it was Ashley, but she was wearing a hat with a veil. Not that I could identify her anyway. I got a much better glimpse of the old man standing on Vincent's other side. About seventy, he was almost bald, and his craggy face was dominated by huge eyebrows which looked as if they were cultivated to compensate for his sparseness on top. That had to be the oil tycoon, the investment banker, the grieving father-in-law. Victor McGahee was among a handful of mourners with umbrellas. Squinting in the rain, I recognized Faye Fluellen despite her sunglasses. No one else looked familiar.

When the priest bowed his head in prayer, I removed my hat out of respect for a woman I had met only once. I thought about our chance encounter and about her deadly car crash a short time later. If only she hadn't taken that one drink too many before she got behind the wheel last Friday. That was a week ago. What did it matter now? She would soon be six feet under, a victim of her own devices.

I thought about sticking around and quizzing the mourners as they left, but I didn't have the heart for it even if they would have cooperated. As I walked around the front of my Ford, I noticed a ticket under the wiper. Flinching at the NO PARKING ZONE sign, I wadded up the sodden ticket, tossed it in the backseat, and drove towards the Chandler Building.

My investigation into Simone's death had been postponed yesterday when I dozed off on my office couch. While asleep, I dreamed I was stuck in the revolving door at Muriel's. I was trying to exit the store, but the door was spinning too fast. Nosy shoppers were crowding around inside the store, and a storm was raging outside. Water was quickly rising in the section of the door where I was trapped. I was soon holding my breath underwater. When I woke, I was gasping for air, and my clothes were damp with sweat. A glance at the wall clock revealed I had slept through the afternoon.

Now, I pulled into Harvey's All-Nighter, a liquor store around the corner from my office building. Before pursuing the Pearson case, I needed a pack of smokes and a pint of inspiration.

EIGHTEEN

I arrived at the office by two. That was usually about quitting time for me on a Friday. I called Lucy, counted ten rings, and hung up. I wasn't quite sure how to restart my investigation. Killing time between calls to Lucy, I took another look at the crime fiction I had been working on. A review of the pages reminded me how badly I'd been squandering my time. With a quick flick of my hand, I swept the stack of papers off my desk. As the floor fan blew them around the office, the door buzzer sounded. I leaped to my feet and frantically tried to gather up the clutter of pages, some still fluttering in the air.

"Be right with you," I said when I heard someone knocking on my office door. The door creaked open, and I looked up to see Nehemiah and Stanley enter the office. Dropping the pages I'd retrieved, I straightened up and warily backed away.

Nehemiah, a broad smile on his face, strode over and turned off the fan. "Working on some crime fiction, Mr. Craven?"

"Not anymore," I responded. "Hard to concentrate with the damn fan blowing my story around." As the papers settled on the floor, he helped me collect them. Stanley stood off to the side, his arms folded across his chest, his hat sitting crookedly on his head. Both men wore dark suits, a dramatic change from their flashy attire at the Charcoal.

"You forgot to number your pages," Nehemiah said as he flipped through the papers he was holding. "Now you're gonna have a problem putting things in order."

"It won't be the first time." I took the pages from him, shuffled them together with mine, and laid them on my desk. "Thanks. Now, what can I do for you?" I cautiously eyed my visitors. Nehemiah went over to the open window. The rain had stopped, and the sky was only partly cloudy now.

"Not much of a breeze, but you got a nice view of the building next door," he said with a smile as he turned the fan back on. "Mind if we have a seat." They both removed their hats at the same time. A large white bandage was wrapped around the top of Stanley's noggin. I gestured towards my customer chairs as I walked behind my desk and sat down.

"I'd introduce you two," said Nehemiah, taking a seat and glancing towards Stanley. Then he looked over at me. "But I understand you already met."

"You owe me a hat, my man," I said as I glared at Stanley, who didn't look quite so intimidating once he was seated. "My fedora got lost during our little confrontation the other night."

"And you owe me somewhere around a hundred bucks, my man," Stanley said. "That's about what you pilfered from my wallet."

"You left out the part where you assaulted me, stole *my* money, and then sold my car to your partner Jerome. I had to pay him fifty dollars to get my vehicle back."

"He says you took the car at gunpoint."

"That son of a bitch took my money and then tried to drive off in my car. I had no choice *but* to pull my gun on him."

"I took about twenty stitches in my damn head because of you." He jerked a thumb towards his bandaged noggin. "There must of been a nail in that stick you smacked me with. And some fucking horse doctor sewed me up without giving me any damn painkillers."

"Nothing more than you deserved for your unprovoked attack on me and your attempted theft of my automobile. My chin's still sore where you hit me. You could've knocked out some teeth."

"Me and Jerome should of broke both your legs before we throwed you in the back of that old truck."

"Enough, gentlemen," Nehemiah said with a loud laugh. "Let's just call it even."

"Why'd you sic him on me, Mr. Wright?" I asked.

Nehemiah calmly turned to Stanley. "Would you care to explain, Stan?"

"It looked like you was hassling Mr. Wright at the Charcoal the other night." He scowled at me. "I'm the bouncer there, so naturally I took it upon myself to straighten you out. And that's exactly what I did."

"Then how come you're the one with the gash in your head?"

"Let's see how you do now you ain't got no big stick with you." Stanley got to his feet. I started to reach for my Colt but, realizing it was in my desk drawer, instead made a mental note to carry it in my shoulder holster at all times.

"Sit down, Stanley," Nehemiah ordered. "You two can settle your differences later. I'm here to talk business." Stanley reluctantly parked himself back in the chair.

"What business would that be, Mr. Wright?" I asked.

"Call me Nehemiah, Mr. Craven. I'd like to hire you to do some snooping for me."

"Call me Sidney," I said, surprised. "I *might* be available as long as I don't have to break any laws."

"No more than usual for your line of work." He smiled. "Can I assume you're no longer employed by Vincent McGahee?"

"That's correct, Nehemiah, but why me?"

"You tracked *me* down. That counts for something. I need someone who has access to white society, Sidney. Today was Simone Pearson's funeral. I want you to find her killer."

NINETEEN

"What makes you think Simone got bumped off?" I asked Nehemiah. I attempted to look calm as I got out my Chesterfields and held out the pack to my two visitors. When they shook their heads, I lit up and slouched back in my chair. Nehemiah took out a cigar and removed the cellophane wrapper, which he crumpled up and deposited in the smoking stand between the two chairs. He took a minute to look the cigar over. Instead of lighting up, however, he stuck it back in his coat pocket.

"When Simone came to see me at the Charcoal last week," Nehemiah finally said, "she told me she was feeling better than ever. And she looked great. She was starting a new movie. So why did she drive her car off some mountain road?"

"You're not the only one asking that question. Let's take things one at a time. Why don't you start at the beginning and tell me about you and Simone?" I reached for my desk drawer, the one that held my office bottle. I paused, deciding against a drink, since I'd have to offer my guests a shot, and I only had two glasses. Instead, I propped my feet on my desk and began listening to Nehemiah's rambling account of his relationship with Simone.

She had remained faithful to her husband for a year and a half after he went off to war, according to Nehemiah. But after long days shooting scenes at the studio, Simone yearned for relief from her nighttime boredom. Eventually she sought diversion in places where she wouldn't run the risk of being recognized by her showbiz acquaintances. She wanted to avoid the hurtful gossip that might result from her frequenting trendy

Hollywood nightspots. In the summer of 1943, she began hanging around Central Avenue bars and jazz joints, which had a mostly colored clientele and were typically considered taboo by respectable whites.

"One night," Nehemiah said, "the band was on break. I noticed a sad-eyed white girl at a table all by herself. I decided to introduce myself. We got off to a shaky start. But we hit it off after a while, and we started dating. Every once in a while Simone joined the band and improvised on standards like *Framed for Love* and *Guilty as Charged*."

Nehemiah stood up and walked back over to the window. He seemed reluctant to continue as he gazed outside. He finally looked my way and said, "When Simone got pregnant at the beginning of the year, there was only one way out. I took her to a back-alley clinic run by some colored doctor. He did abortions. That quack ought to be run out of town. I think the bastard used a coat hanger on Simone. She got a goddamn infection from the botched operation and wound up in the hospital with pneumonia." Nehemiah seemed miserable enough to throw himself out my ten-story window. But for now he resumed his narrative.

"Simone couldn't work. She got replaced on the movie she just started shooting. When she got better, she showed up at Empire and complained to the director for giving her part to another girl. The damn studio fired her. I saw a tabloid story that said Simone was drunk when she told off the director. I showed her the story, but she laughed it off. Said it was just Hollywood gossip. I worried about her." Nehemiah moved away from the window and went back to his chair.

Simone went on numerous auditions at other studios, Nehemiah recalled, but was never cast in any roles. She thought she was being blackballed because of her clash with the director. Her downward spiral in showbiz was frustrating for her. As their relationship began falling apart, Nehemiah noticed she was hitting the bottle. "I wondered if Simone had family troubles," he said. "But she would never talk about her life on Beverly Glen."

"Maybe she wanted to keep her two worlds separate," I said, just to hear my voice.

"Maybe," Nehemiah said with a frown. "Anyway, Simone hung around the Charcoal, but our little fling was definitely over. She got friendly with the regulars. There was talk about Simone sleeping around some. When she was drinking, she maybe wasn't always too particular who she left with at closing time. I heard she never went back to Beverly Glen with anyone. It had to be their place or a hotel. I know she sometimes left her little Packard parked across the street overnight. Simone was afraid to drive herself home when it got late. And she wouldn't even let me drop her off. Said she was worried about what her neighbors might think. She spent some nights on the couch in the back room at the Charcoal. She would drive home in the morning, and I might not see her around for days."

Nehemiah stood up and started pacing in front of my desk. He brought out his cigar and a wooden match which he lit on his thumbnail. He was soon puffing away. "Simone started pestering me to get her a gun for protection." He shook his head. "She was worried about prowlers."

"Can't really blame her," I said. "Wasn't she living alone in that big house?"

"Yeah, but I didn't think a gun was a smart idea, so I sat her down and tried to talk some sense into her. That's when I noticed needle tracks on her arm. I found out it was Loretta who showed her how to shoot up. She's one of my Delights. I wanted to kill the bitch. Loretta's lucky I didn't find her while I was still pissed off. I told Simone she wasn't getting any more handouts from me. I was helping her out with money, but I wasn't about to pay for her drug habit." Nehemiah paused and sat down again. He elbowed Stanley, who was slumped in his chair with his eyes shut. The big guy sat up, yawned, and took such a deep breath that I imagined myself gasping for whatever air was left in the room.

"I stopped paying much attention to Simone," Nehemiah said. "I got a nightclub to run, and it was easier just to let her be. I told Stanley to try and keep predators away from her." He nodded at the big man. "After a while, I couldn't help noticing that Simone was becoming lax about her appearance and her clothes. Didn't comb her hair. Lost weight. Got to where she couldn't perform with the band anymore." Nehemiah looked sadly into the distance as if he were attempting to conjure up a vision of his old girlfriend.

"Then she just went into hiding," he said. "Stayed gone for weeks. Finally turned up with the news about how she quit heroin. Said she went to some revival meeting and got born again and ain't touched the stuff since. Now, I believe in the power of God, but I know you don't get cured from no drug addiction overnight. I was hooked myself. When I laughed at her, she told me the truth. She spent two weeks in some private hospital before she kicked her habit. It takes time to get over your craving for the needle. After her fall from grace, Simone was ready to redeem herself." His voice began rising like a preacher's during a Sunday sermon. "She finally rid herself of her demons and was about to reclaim her rightful place in the world."

"Amen, brother," Stanley mumbled. The room was quiet for a minute except for the humming of the floor fan and traffic noise from the street down below. I lit another cigarette, and Nehemiah puffed some more on his cheap cigar.

"Her husband just returned from the war," he said. "Maybe he found out about us. Then he got some righteous indignation and murdered her." Nehemiah looked at me and shrugged. "I know *something* ain't right. The story in the *Mirror* said Simone got into a ruckus with you at that ritzy clothing store. What really happened?"

"I confronted her after catching her shoplifting some undergarments. I never laid a hand on her. She slapped me and, uh, kicked me."

"That's what I'm talking about. That don't sound like the Simone I knew."

"Her husband said she shoplifted before and threw tantrums when she got nabbed. But he always managed to get it hushed up. Maybe she had a dark side you didn't know about."

Nehemiah stood up again, stuck his cigar in his mouth, and pulled out a fat wallet. He removed two bills and tossed them onto my desk. They were hundreds. "I don't care what the husband says. I want you to look into it. I owe her that much."

"Will do, Nehemiah," I said as I leaned forward and quickly closed my twitching fingers around the money. "Know the name of the hospital where Simone stayed?"

"Believe she said it was in Burbank or Glendale. Told me it was on the q.t. And that's all she would tell me."

"Did you ever get Simone a gun?" I asked.

"I thought she was imagining things. She didn't hardly trust anybody.

But I bought her a small-caliber handgun just to ease her mind. It was a silver Colt pocket automatic with a six-round magazine. Stanley took her to a firing range and showed her how to shoot. Looks like she was right about needing a gun. But I guess she never got the chance to use it. When the time came, maybe she wasn't able to pull the trigger, or else she got caught by surprise. I don't know what the hell happened. I just know somebody knocked her off and fixed it to look like it was her own fault."

I saw no reason to disagree with my client's assertion. "I'll keep you informed of any developments," I promised, standing up and stashing his payment in my wallet. I gave him my card and we shook hands. Then Nehemiah shook Stanley by the shoulder. The large guy had been snoring for some time. Sleepily rising from his chair, he gently placed his derby on his bandaged head. He followed Nehemiah, who had already donned his fedora, and they both exited the office.

I stubbed out my cigarette and called Lucy again, but this time the line was busy. I wasn't crazy about working for two different clients on the same case, but there really wasn't a conflict of interest. Both Nehemiah Wright and Wesley Renfro wanted me to show that Simone Pearson's death *wasn't* accidental. Nehemiah was convinced it was murder and wanted me to find the culprit. Renfro thought it was suicide and wanted me to find evidence that would get his Uptowner insurance company off the hook for thirty grand. If it looked like suicide, Uptowner could refuse to pay out even a penny. Vincent McGahee would have to sue for his money. I didn't know if it was murder or suicide. Maybe it *was* just an accident. After thinking it over for a minute, I decided it didn't matter. I was looking for the truth. I pulled open the desk drawer to get my bottle of whiskey. As I uncapped the bottle, the buzzer sounded, and I heard approaching footsteps. I took a quick gulp and then put the pint away.

TWENTY

"Come on in," I said. The door opened and Faye Fluellen, in a colorful summer dress, matching hat and high heels, strolled into my office and took a seat in one of my customer chairs. A small purse on a long string hung from her shoulder. She was wearing sunglasses and looked as if she just stepped off a movie set. She had changed outfits since her visit to the cemetery, where she wore black. Since then the weather had changed as well. Her new outfit matched the sunny day.

"What brings you here, Mrs. Wilkins? Didn't think your husband let you out of the house."

"He can't keep me cooped up every minute," she said. "Now, I want that free vacuum cleaner you promised but never delivered." I shrugged and she laughed. Her split lip was healing, and the bruise on her cheek had faded. "Just like a salesman," she added. "Can't trust none of 'em."

"I'm not a salesman."

"I know, Mr. Craven, but after what I read about you in the *Mirror*, I'm not sure I can trust you."

"Why would you want to?"

"I can't go to the police, but I thought I should tell some kinda detective what I know about Simone Pearson. So I looked up your address in the phone book, Mr. Dime Detective. And here I am." She seemed proud of herself. If I just stayed put, maybe enough people would parade into my office with information about Simone to solve the case for me. Faye got up, tiptoed back across the room, and opened the office door. Lifting her sunglasses, she peeked into the waiting room. With her shades back in place, she quietly returned to her seat.

"Checking for eavesdroppers?" I asked. "If anyone enters that room, the buzzer will sound, tipping us off."

"When I stepped off the elevator, two colored gents got on. I didn't get a very good look, but I could swear I saw at least one of 'em somewhere before. They're probably up to no good."

I reached into my top drawer, brought out my gun, and set it down on my desk. "If any troublemakers come in here," I said with a straight face, "I'm ready for 'em."

"You've got a weapon!" she said in astonishment.

"I've even got a permit for it, and I can assure you I know how to pull the trigger and everything. Just calm down." She seemed as jittery as a blind man jaywalking during rush hour in downtown L.A.

"I went to Simone's funeral," Faye announced.

"How'd you get invited?"

"I called up Simone's husband to offer my condolences, and he asked me if I'd like to attend. I haven't been able to get her off my mind. I think I know why she drove off that road and killed herself. She was being blackmailed and was frightened her husband would find out. It's partly my fault. I feel terrible about it, and I've just got to tell someone."

"What the hell are you talking about?"

"Way back in January, Simone calls me. She got herself pregnant. It had to be that trumpet player Nehemiah, because she used to hang out at them South Central joints. Simone wouldn't say. She wants to know can I recommend some doctor that can fix it for her. I told her I couldn't talk, since my husband was home, and he don't like me on the phone. I said she should call me later. She never called back, but I called *her* a few days later and she told me she found a doctor and it was all taken care of."

I reached for my cigarettes. Faye started sobbing, so I got up, walked around my desk, and sat down in the chair next to hers. I took out my handkerchief and handed it to her. She removed her sunglasses and dabbed gently at her eyes. I recoiled when I saw her left eye which was nearly swollen shut. I reached over and placed my hand on her shoulder in a clumsy attempt to comfort her.

Pushing me away, she said, "Even if you didn't get fresh with Simone at Muriel's, I don't like being touched by you or any strange man." Being brutalized by her husband was apparently all right. Handkerchief in one hand and sunglasses in the other, she continued her story.

Not long before Simone called about her predicament, Faye's stuntman husband Ted had lost his job with the studio. Faye herself was forced to stop working within days when she fell down her apartment stairway and broke her arm. With both husband and wife unemployed, bills started piling up.

"I talked over Simone's situation with Ted," Faye said. "We saw it as a chance to get the bill collectors off our backs. We were desperate. I'm ashamed to say what I done, but I offered to sell the lowdown on Simone to Bert Brenley."

Always sniffing around the studios for a scoop, Brenley was known to most of the Hollywood film community. The sleazy reporter probably drooled at the thought of getting the goods on a popular actress. But he haggled with Faye over the value of her salacious info. When Ted got on the phone and threatened to break Brenley's fat neck, they finally agreed on a dollar amount. Faye coughed up the pertinent details about Simone's affair with her trumpet player. Brenley must have checked it out, because several days later she found an envelope stuffed with money in her mailbox. Faye anxiously began reading each day's *Mirror* from cover to cover but never found any mention of the scandal.

"Then, I got another call from Simone," Faye said. "She asked me if I blabbed about her pregnancy and abortion to Bert Brenley. Of course, I denied it. She said he somehow found out about everything and was blackmailing her. The *Mirror* was gonna run the story unless..." She paused. "You know what Brenley done? The tricky bastard got hold of a picture of Simone and her boyfriend and mailed a copy to her. He said the photo was going on the front page, and the whole trashy story would be in his tabloid unless she came up with the blackmail money. That's when my husband came home, and I had to hang up." Faye blew her nose on my handkerchief.

"Did Simone come up with the hush money?" I asked.

"She must of, because the *Mirror* never printed the damn story. Me and Ted wondered how she managed it, because I remember reading about her getting fired by Empire. Her father-in-law's a millionaire, but it probably would of been too awkward for her to go to him. Know what I mean? Anyway, we had money worries of our own. What we got from Brenley helped us survive until Ted found another job." When she paused, I stood up, took a seat on the edge of my desk, and lit a cigarette. I thought about asking her how much she got for betraying Simone, but she started sobbing again.

"You know," she finally continued, "Simone's husband just got back from overseas. I figure she was scared out of her mind he'd get wind of her shenanigans. I know it's almost impossible for *me* to keep secrets from *my* husband. She probably just fell apart. I mean, not showing up at the studio for her new movie, then the weird shoplifting thing, and crashing her car. She just wasn't in her right mind." Faye shook her head. "I blame that son of a bitch Brenley for what happened to Simone, but I guess I'm an accomplice. I feel like shit about the whole goddamn thing."

I balked at her sudden use of profanity, but she was obviously being truthful about her feelings. Putting on her shades, she stood up and brushed the wrinkles from her dress. I got to my feet and mashed out my cigarette in the smoking stand. She handed over my handkerchief, and I gave her my card, which she stuffed inside her purse.

"Guess what?" she said. "I called Brenley right after I read his story in the *Mirror* about Simone's run-in with you at Muriel's and her disappearance. I told him I knew he was a blackmailer."

"What did he say?"

"He figured as much. I said if something happened to Simone and his tabloid ever ran the story about her and Nehemiah, I'd go to the cops. Now she's dead. Brenley better let her rest in peace." Faye glanced at her watch. "Gotta go. Hope my taxi's still waiting. You know, my husband's a night watchman now. Ted was sleeping when I left to go to the funeral earlier today, and he was gone when I got back to the apartment. So I decided to come over here. Ted leaves whenever he wants to, so why can't I?" She smiled, slid her sunglasses down her nose, and gave me a wink with her good eye. "If I didn't know how much he loved me, I might think he was sneaking off to see another woman."

"You sure he didn't knock you down the stairs that time you broke your arm? You should call the cops the next time that lummox lays a hand on you."

She walked towards the door, then paused, but she hadn't been listening. "Last time I talked to Simone was a week ago when she called me up and told me her agent got her an audition. She was making a comeback. What a shame."

"You wouldn't happen to know her agent's name, would you?"

"Sure." She laughed. "Harrison Hammerman. Who could forget a name like that once you hear it? Looks like me and Simone are *both* retired from showbiz now." As she turned and walked out the door, I got a good whiff of her perfume, which floated on the air like a memory of better times.

TWENTY-ONE

About midnight on Friday, I was awakened by a deafening whistle blast. Ten minutes later workers poured through the gates of the Tiptop Aviation plant in Torrance. Formerly a maker of auto parts, Tiptop was converted after the start of the war into an assembly plant for airplane parts. Lucy worked there. With her rivet gun, she fastened together metal parts used on military planes.

I climbed out of my Ford which was parked outside the plant. I sat on the hood and held up a big cardboard sign that said: LUCY. Men and women, most wearing gray work uniforms, but some in blue jeans and tee shirts, trudged past me into the parking lot. Workers on the next shift were filing into the plant. A long-legged blonde, maybe forty, dressed in a shapeless uniform and carrying a suitcase, walked up to the Ford.

"Hey, Sidney," she said, smiling. "I'm your blind date."

"If you can't see, how'd you know it was me?"

"That's an old one," she said. "Stole it from the Marx Brothers, didn't you?"

"Can't remember." I laughed as I hopped off the hood and took her luggage.

"You look better in person than you did on the front page of the *Mirror*," she said as I heaved her suitcase, along with the cardboard sign, into my trunk and next to my overnight bag.

"Thanks a lot," I said. When we got into the car, I realized I had my hat on and tossed the gray fedora into the backseat. Having retired my suit until

Monday, I was wearing casual trousers and a sports shirt. "Ready to gamble away your hard-earned cash?"

"No, but I'm ready to gamble away yours," Lucy replied with a laugh. We joined the cluster of cars with tired workers heading home. But *we* weren't going home. Our plan was to take Pacific Coast Highway north and then turn onto Topanga Canyon Boulevard, which would take us over the Santa Monica Mountains and into the San Fernando Valley. Then we were going to drive through the night to Reno. She'd wanted to take a shorter route to the Valley, but I convinced her that getting there was half the fun. Just leave the driving to me. What could go wrong?

Lucy had decided she wanted to spend a weekend away from L.A. She'd been to Reno earlier in the year for her divorce. Her brother had bought her a round-trip plane ticket. "It was cold and rainy when I went before," she said. "This time I wanna have some laughs."

She'd called from a phone booth at work just as I was about to leave my office on Friday afternoon. Faye Fluellen's perfume was still in the air. Lucy had brought up her idea for a Reno getaway, but she figured it was just a pipe dream. "Damn gas stamps!" she said. "No way you'll have enough for a long drive." I told her not to think twice about Uncle Sam's gas rationing because I had enough gas ration stamps in my glove box to buy fuel for our entire trip—and then some.

A while back I had tracked down a cheating husband, his arm around his girlfriend, and snapped a photo of the pair coming down the stairs in some dingy hotel. The guy was a big-shot politician who was running for reelection. Naturally he wanted to avoid the tabloid headlines that would ensue when his wife filed for a divorce.

For not reporting back to his spouse on his infidelity, I was offered a bribe I couldn't resist. He said he'd keep me supplied with extra gas stamps. Maybe he knew someone on the local rationing board. I didn't ask any questions. But I figured my days of carefree driving wouldn't last forever. He'd probably cut off my stamp supply after election day. Then I'd have to rely on the stingy amount of gas stamps the government doled out. I'd be able to buy about enough gas to drive around town, but no more road trips. I planned to enjoy myself while I could.

Reno was some five hundred miles away. In nighttime traffic, we might be able to make it in about ten hours—if I ignored the wartime speed limit of thirty-five *and* my car didn't break down.

By the time we reached Topanga Canyon, we'd run out of small talk and Lucy was yawning. "I can't keep my eyes open," she said. "I was even too tired to take a shower after my shift ended. I just tossed my coveralls and welding gloves into my locker and headed for the exit. I couldn't wait to get some fresh air." Then, climbing into the backseat, she almost kicked me in the head with one of her oversized work shoes. "Wake me when we get to Reno. Uh-oh, I just squashed something. Your hat." She started laughing. "You don't believe in omens, do you?" She couldn't stop laughing.

"No way. You need some sleep." I didn't know how comfortable Lucy would be in the back seat, but she didn't complain. Within minutes, she was snoring softly.

I made good time on the two-lane canyon road and was soon up in the mountains. An occasional vehicle, its headlights briefly obscuring my vision, would suddenly come towards me from around a bend in the road and then shoot past. It was a cool night with a sky full of stars. We'd both rolled up our windows, but now I cranked mine about halfway down, then lit a cigarette and relaxed behind the wheel. I had the north lane all to myself—with nothing but darkness in my wake—until another car came roaring up behind me and began tailgating my sedan.

"Get a move on!" the driver yelled as he leaned out his window. "I ain't got all night!" With the car's headlights reflecting in my rearview mirror, I couldn't get a good look at the vehicle or its driver. When he began impatiently blasting his horn, I stepped on the gas but had to brake quickly on the next curve. We were on a winding stretch of roadway with a mountainside on our right. Since there was no shoulder between the road and the mountain, I couldn't pull over and let him by. He suddenly rammed into my rear bumper, and my head was jolted back. The cigarette I'd stuck in the corner of my mouth went flying into the back of the car, where I soon heard Lucy scrambling around.

"Ouch!" she said. "What's the big idea? Why'd you throw your cigarette back here?"

"It was an accident."

"What the hell's going on?" She peered over the top of the front seat and flipped the cigarette out my window just as the guy hit his horn again.

"Some lunatic is trying to run us off the road," I told her.

"Why doesn't he just pass us?" Lucy asked as she climbed into the front seat. I stuck my arm out the window and motioned for him to go by, but just then lights appeared up ahead, and a car came around a turn and sped past in the opposite direction.

"That's why," I said.

The guy behind me gave his horn an angry blast. "You trying to get me killed?" he shouted.

"What are we gonna do?" Lucy asked. Another horn blast pierced the night.

"The guy's probably drunk—on his way home from a party." I rolled my window all the way up. "Now we don't have to listen to the loudmouth."

"Just our luck to get stuck in front of him."

He rammed my car again and we were both jerked backwards. I tightened my grip on the steering wheel as we careened around another curve. Then a section of the road ahead straightened, and I eased off the gas. Now was his chance to pass. Speeding up, he pulled his big car alongside my sedan. When I glanced his way, he veered over and forced me to the right. I slammed on my brakes. As he roared past, my Ford's two right wheels skidded off the road, and my car went up the side of the steep mountain.

The car teetered at a dangerous angle for a minute and then rolled over onto the driver's side. And it kept on rolling. The car turned upside down, then onto the passenger side, and finally upright again. Rocking wildly, it came to rest in the lane for oncoming traffic. Inside the tumbling car, we had tried to brace ourselves but were tossed about like two mannequins.

"Are you okay?" I asked when Lucy stopped screaming. We were scrunched together on the passenger side. After we untangled ourselves, I moved back behind the wheel.

"My head hurts," she said, groaning, "but I think I'll live. That scared the hell out of me."

"I want to see how much damage that roll did to my car." My window had a long crack in it and was hard to roll down. I started to get out. The door was stuck but opened with a shove. My Ford was only a couple of feet from a battered guardrail. Just beyond the guardrail was a steep descent.

"Don't you think we should get the hell out of here before another car comes along?" Lucy said reasonably. "We're in the wrong lane."

Trying to get my thoughts together, I shook my head. "Why didn't *I* think of that?" I smiled crookedly. "Guess I'm a little rattled." I left the door ajar and turned the ignition key. The car had stalled during its tumble, and now I couldn't get it started. "Maybe it's flooded. Get behind the wheel, and I'll push." After I carefully stepped out, Lucy slid over and shifted into neutral. Holding the door open, I leaned forward and pushed. But my Ford must have been on an incline because the car started rolling backwards.

Lucy jammed on the brakes. "Let *me* try." To my astonishment, she started the Ford immediately. Up around the bend a car was coming our way. I could see headlights bouncing off the road and braced myself for a head-on collision.

"Drive!" I hollered, closing the door and jumping onto the running board. Lucy shifted into gear and floored it. The wheels spun, and I could smell burning rubber. The old Ford began sliding sideways before lurching forward into the north lane just as the approaching car swooped by and buffeted us with a blast of dusty air. Lucy quickly braked, put it in neutral, and scooted over. As the car started rolling backwards again, I climbed in and slammed the door. I stepped on the brakes, then shifted into first, and gave it some gas. Once again we were headed north. I adjusted the cracked rearview mirror. "My door still works and so do the headlights. You still wanna go to Reno?"

Moving over, she leaned against me, and I breathed in a pleasant mixture of sweat and perfume. "We're not gonna let this little mishap ruin our trip, are we?" she said with a laugh, but I could feel her shaking. She wasn't the only jittery one.

"You know, that's probably gonna be the high point of our trip."

"I can live with that."

"Sure you're all right?"

"Got a bump on my head and probably some bruises."

"I'm sore all over," I said.

"Think we should report that guy?"

"What kind of car was he driving?"

"I don't know, but I think it was red," she said. "I was sort of distracted."

"That's more than *I* noticed. You know, I thought I was being tailed by a red car a few days ago. Probably just a coincidence. Lots of red cars in L.A." We drove in silence for a while.

"Now that my heart rate's almost back to normal," Lucy finally said, "I gotta try to get some sleep, or I'm gonna be too tired when we get to Reno." She disappeared behind the front seat. "Next time we get some crazy guy following us, give me a warning. And not with your cigarette butt." She laughed. I liked Lucy's easygoing style. Maybe it was a style I should try out for myself.

When we reached the Valley, I stopped for gas at a service station. I was about the only customer on a slow night. I checked out the damage to my car while the attendant worked the pump. The passenger door was stuck shut, and the window—a spider web of cracks—wouldn't budge. At least the driver's door and window worked. The windshield and rear window looked okay, and both the headlights and taillights had survived. The trunk and hood still opened and closed, but one of the wings on the hood ornament had broken off. Two hubcaps were missing. The secondhand Ford didn't have any side mirrors when I bought it. The body had some scrapes and dents, but it could have been worse.

"Looks like it's been rolled," the attendant said.

I nodded and asked him to check under the hood in case something was awry. The radiator had a slow leak, and he added some water. Then he replaced the fan belt. He showed me the old one, which had a slice almost all the way through it. "Your fan belt was being held together by threads. Maybe some lame mechanic installed a defective belt, or maybe it was purposely cut. If your fan belt breaks, your engine will overheat, and you'll find yourself stranded somewhere. You're lucky we caught it in time." He pulled out a pocketknife. Using a sawing motion he demonstrated how the belt could be slit. "Got any enemies?"

"Who doesn't?" I answered. I paid up, and he took a handful of my gas stamps.

Lucy was still sleeping when I pulled back onto the road. Once I hit the highway, I drove north past orange groves, farms, and old wooden derricks in oil fields that looked abandoned. The smell of oil and stagnant water seeped in through my partly opened window. Bet old man McGahee was glad he didn't have to sniff that aroma anymore. He'd moved up in the world.

I lit a cigarette and tried to figure out who would want to cut my fan belt or try to run me off the road. Maybe someone in a red car didn't want me looking into Simone Pearson's death and wanted to scare the hell out of me so I'd back off. It didn't make much sense. My investigation wasn't really going anywhere. I tried to relax and enjoy the trip.

Nighttime travel wasn't the best way to appreciate the scenery, but there weren't any bottlenecks either. I tried to keep my speed at just about fifty. When I drove any faster, my car would start to rattle and shake. Lucy woke up about daybreak and said, "Let me know when we catch up to the guy in the big red car. I wanna give him a piece of my mind."

"You and me both." I laughed and lit another cigarette. She was asleep again when I turned near Sacramento and took the highway northeast towards the Sierra Nevadas. The sun was climbing high in the sky by the time we reached the mountain range. I woke Lucy, and we both marveled at the endless growth of pine trees and the towering mountain peaks. She hadn't really appreciated the view from a plane and agreed it was worth a close-up look. Lucy nodded off again but was in the front seat and wide awake as we crossed into Nevada, north of Lake Tahoe. About an hour later, we entered downtown Reno. We turned onto Virginia Street and drove under the famed arch with the sign: THE BIGGEST LITTLE CITY IN THE WORLD.

It was early afternoon, cool, and windy. "It looks like we picked the right time of year to visit Reno," she said. We drove past casinos, their neon lights welcoming tourists around the clock. We checked into a cheap hotel down the street, just beyond the big hotels and casinos. Lucy proceeded to the bathroom while I stretched out on one of the two beds in our room. When I woke two hours later, Lucy wasn't around. I found her short note on the dresser: "Gone gambling."

Shaved, showered, and in my weekend clothes, I checked my wallet. I had brought Nehemiah's generous cash payment with me. I walked up the street and stopped at the first casino, the Winning Streak. Even in the daytime, noisy gamblers were crowded around craps tables and roulette wheels. Others were feeding coins into slot machines. I wondered how many had come to Reno for quick divorces after gambling on marriages and losing. Now they'd decided to stick around to wager on other games of chance. Unable to find Lucy, I walked past the poker tables, took a seat at one of the blackjack tables, and ordered a whiskey. I bought some chips from the dealer. Placing moderate bets, I played a number of hands but called it quits after I lost five bucks. I wandered over to the craps tables.

An attractive blonde in a wispy orange dress, sheer nylons, and high heels caught my eye. I almost didn't recognize Lucy without her work clothes. I joined her just in time to see her roll a seven and lose a huge bet. Quickly wielding his rake, the stickman at the table pushed away her stacks of cash and chips.

"I was on a winning streak until you showed up," she said, smiling as she looped her arm around my waist. "Now you gotta make it up to me."

She held out her hand and I gave her a ten. Between sips of her beer, she placed several careless bets, and within fifteen minutes she'd lost my ten. She ordered another beer, and I gave her another ten. When that ten was gone, I talked her into playing the slots. My money would last longer that way. We wandered up the street and tried our luck at other casinos. Urged on by a rowdy crowd, Lucy rolled a dozen winners at one of the craps tables. With drinks on the house everywhere—and no clocks anywhere—time flew by. We gambled the day away.

After a late supper at a casino restaurant, we returned to our hotel room. It was about dusk. I followed her inside and closed the door. The air conditioning was on full blast and the room was chilly. She turned and gave me a quick kiss. I put my arms around her and held her close. We kissed for a long time. Finally she pulled away and gestured towards the beds. "Which one should we try out?" she asked with a laugh.

"You choose." While I fumbled with my shirt buttons, Lucy kicked off her shoes, pulled her dress over her head, and peeled off her nylons and undergarments. Just about the time my zipper snagged, she hopped into the bed near the window and pulled up the covers. After a minute I joined her.

Later on we found a movie theater wedged between two casinos. The marquee announced a special screening of Simone Pearson's film *Life Is Just a Gamble*. We missed the newsreel but arrived in time to catch a short promo for U.S. war bonds. As we found seats, Hollywood starlets in sailor uniforms paraded around on the screen. They were holding up signs: BUY BONDS IN THIS THEATER. I couldn't help wondering if any of them had become strangler victims.

The black-and-white feature was about three years old. There was no question how different Simone looked on the big screen than she did in person at Muriel's. Larger than life, she wasn't exactly beautiful. Maybe her nose was too large and her chin too long; nonetheless, she was attractive. Her sense of comic timing was uncanny, and when she delivered her lines, which—thanks to some clever screenwriter—were witty and amusing, she repeatedly drew laughter from the audience. Simone stole every scene she was in. She reminded me of Carole Lombard, who was killed two years ago in a plane crash. My heart sank when I realized such talented actresses would never again make another film that would bring together so many strangers in a dark theater to share some laughs.

TWENTY-TWO

"I'll hold," I said into the phone as I glanced down at the photo of Simone and her two sidekicks in their military uniforms. Back in the office on Monday afternoon, I was still recuperating from my Reno adventure with Lucy. We didn't allow the troubling mishap with my car to dampen our trip. After gambling away some more of my money Sunday morning, we departed for L.A. We arrived back in the big city late in the evening. I'd needed a dose of R and R along with some female companionship. I haven't worked so hard on a case since before the war.

After a five-minute wait, Bert Brenley finally picked up the phone at the other end. "Hello."

"Hey, Brenley. I'm boycotting your sleazy tabloid, *and* I'm going to the police." I kept my voice calm, and tried to control my temper.

"*What?* Who's this?"

"Never mind. I know you were blackmailing Simone Pearson, you son of a bitch."

"You must be hallucinating."

"When the cops find out that you're even more unsavory than the stories you write, they'll throw your butt in jail, you lousy bastard." I could feel myself unraveling and took a deep breath. "Were you still putting the squeeze on Simone at the time of her death?"

"Listen, you anonymous moron! I'll sue your ass for slander. I'll take your house, your car, your dog, your cat—"

"You couldn't sue anyone for slander, because no one could ever accuse you of something you're not guilty of. You're lower than the lowest cockroach. You're a piece of shit that even the nastiest flies wouldn't touch." When I heard the dial tone, I stopped shouting and hung up the phone.

With a shaky hand, I reached for the fifth of whiskey on my desk, but it was empty. In the half-hour since arriving at the office, I'd been draining the bottle's contents as I prepared to tell off Brenley. I didn't know if I was angrier with him for writing half-truths about me in the *Mirror* or for blackmailing Simone.

Next, I called Harrison Hammerman's office, but the Hollywood agent's secretary said he'd left for the day.

"It's only three o'clock," I said.

"Thanks for the time check," she responded. "Now, may I take a message for Mr. Hammerman?"

"Yeah, remind him he's an agent and not a banker." I hung up. I thought maybe Simone had confided something to her agent that might be helpful. Then I grabbed the phone book and started flipping through it. I was looking for hospitals in Burbank, Glendale, and even Pasadena. I made a number of calls without success. Putting my finger under the next number, I dialed the Wamsley Medical Center.

"May I please speak with a patient named Simone Pearson?" I asked when the receptionist answered the phone.

"One moment, please," she said. Drumming my fingers on the desk, I waited impatiently. Finally someone with authority in his voice got on the phone.

"This is Dr. Wamsley. Who's calling?"

"Detective Waven, LAPD."

"Are you asking about Simone Pearson, the actress?"

"Of course."

"If you're really a detective, you should know she's dead."

"Was she ever a patient in your mental ward?"

"What did you say your name was?"

"Waven," I said, and spelled it for him.

"You'll need an appropriate warrant before I can release any confidential information about any of our present or former patients."

"Couldn't you just waive the red tape for once?"

"No, Detective Waven, I can't waive—"

I hung up. That had to be the place: an out-of-the-way hospital where someone might go for an appendectomy or perhaps a little detoxification. Guess I'd have to resort to some legwork. But first things first. The gray fedora I had found in my closet wasn't working for me. The color didn't match my favorite suit now at the dry cleaners. I marched down the hallway to see if Wanda could fix me up.

Fifteen minutes later I strolled back to my office under a new lid, which—after some haggling—I'd purchased at a discount. When I opened my waiting-room door, I had a visitor. Her legs curled under her, Tina Ferrante was perched on my couch and thumbing through an old magazine. She was wearing black slacks and a pink blouse. She had short brown hair with long bangs that she brushed aside with her finger as she glanced up.

"I like you better without the blonde wig and all the movie makeup," I said. "You look great, Miss Ferrante."

"Wish I could say the same about you." She laughed.

"I haven't been getting enough sleep lately." I unlocked my office door and motioned for her to join me inside. She picked out a customer chair while I tossed my new fedora next to my old one on the desk and made a mental note to buy a hat rack. I offered her a cigarette, tried to light a match on my thumbnail, gave up, and used the side of my desk. When both our cigarettes were lit, I sat on the edge of my desk. "How's the movie business?"

"I'm done shooting my scene for today. I only have a small part, you know."

"I guess I should be mad at you and your director for repeating to Bert Brenley everything I told you about Simone over at Empire."

"Mr. Seymour said we should cooperate with him. After all, he's a reporter."

"Did Brenley promise to give you some free publicity in his gossip column? Maybe promote your new movie?"

"He may have mentioned something along those lines. This is Hollywood. I gotta take whatever opportunity comes my way." She smiled sweetly.

"How can I help you, Miss Ferrante?"

"I'm being followed, Mr. Craven, and I'm afraid to go home."

"Why don't you stay at Mr. Seymour's place? He'll protect you."

"Get serious for a minute," she replied.

"I thought the two of you—"

"I can't just move in with him. He's married. We're trying to be discreet."

"If *I* could figure it out."

"You're a detective. Actually, you're the only one I know in that racket."

"Who's following you, Miss Ferrante?"

"I think it's…the strangler. That's why I can't go home. All his victims have been killed in their apartments. I don't want to be next."

"Sounds like you need a bodyguard," I said, "not a detective. Can't you stay with a friend?"

"I don't feel safe anywhere."

"Did you get a good look at this guy?"

"No, but I've seen him lurking around my apartment building. He stays in the shadows."

"Maybe he's just a derelict or a wino."

"I'm not taking any chances, Mr. Craven."

"How'd you get here?"

"By streetcar."

"Think he followed you?"

"I'm not sure."

"Why don't I give you a ride home and make sure you get in your apartment safe and sound?"

She sighed and frowned. "That sounds okay. Unless you're the strangler." She laughed nervously. We snuffed out our cigarette butts in the smoking stand. I took my shoulder holster from my desk drawer and put it on. After checking my gun, I got into my suit coat and grabbed my new hat.

"I feel safer already," she said with a smile.

On our way over to her place, I explained to Tina why my Ford needed some body work. Then I reassured her I really was a good driver. "I've just had a streak of bad luck, but I got a feeling my luck's about to change."

Tina Ferrante lived in an older three-story apartment building on Franklin Avenue near Western, not too far from Empire Studios. I parked on the street out front. We walked under an arched entrance and along a concrete walkway that led to the building's courtyard. Tina pointed to her apartment. "It's the one in the corner, on the second floor." Paint was peeling from the side of the building. Two lonely palm trees stood on a patch of brown grass in the center of the courtyard.

"Nothing suspicious looking yet," I said as we climbed the stairs and proceeded along the balcony. It was nearly five. Other tenants would be returning from work soon. Once inside her small apartment, I searched the usual places: in the closets, behind the shower curtain, under the bed. "Nothing." I tried to sound reassuring. "Keep the door locked and don't let any strangers in. Call Seymour. He can give you a ride to work in the morning, unless you think he might be—"

"Stop it," she said with a smile. "What do I owe you?"

"How about free tickets to the premiere of your new movie?"

"I might be able to swing that. After all, I know the director."

I went down the stairs and walked back to my car. The neighborhood, just the other side of the railway tracks, was crowded with tenements. There were plenty of parking lots and shadowy alleyways, places where seedy characters could loiter more or less unnoticed.

As I started to open my car door, something caught my eye. The sun was glinting off a wine bottle, upended at the moment by a vagrant taking a belt while standing in the alleyway between two buildings down the street. I decided to check him out. When he saw me heading his way, he dropped the bottle and hustled down the alley.

"Hey, fella," I shouted, "can I have a word with you?" I chased him through the alley. I was right behind him when he rounded the building and began climbing a wobbly chain-link fence. He got about halfway up before the high fence toppled over, taking him with it. As I approached him, he clutched the fence and tried to kick me with both feet.

"Come on, buddy," I said, "stand up like a man." Avoiding his kicks, I pried loose his fingers. Gripping the collar of his raggedy jacket, I jerked him upright. We stumbled a few steps in an awkward dance as the fence slowly righted itself behind us. We were standing in the building's parking area. He was a tall rangy guy with a scraggly beard. His worn-out, loose-fitting clothes reeked of alcohol.

"What's the big idea?" I demanded, holding onto his jacket and shaking him to emphasize my point. "You're scaring people in the neighborhood by sneaking around in alleyways."

"What the hell do you think you're doing?" he yelled.

"Talking to a wino with a bad attitude." I released his jacket and he staggered backwards.

"You're gonna be one sorry SOB." He sounded more angry than drunk.

"Strangled any starlets lately?" I asked with a smirk. He stepped forward and took a big swing at me, but I easily dodged out of the way. As his momentum carried him past me, I resisted the temptation to throw a punch of my own. Before he could recover his balance, however, I gave him a shove, and he went headfirst into the fence and tumbled to the ground.

I felt guilty pushing around a guy in his depraved condition. But only for a minute. "Take it easy, man. Neighbors are complaining about you. They think you might be the strangler."

"Who the hell *are* you?" He rubbed the top of his head as he sat against the fence.

"I can tell you're just a harmless drunk," I said, ignoring his question. "Here, I'll give you a whole dollar." I reached into my pocket. "Get yourself another bottle of cheap wine. Just take it somewhere else."

"Fuck you, asshole!" The conversation had quickly deteriorated.

"On second thought, I'm not giving you a *dime*. Why don't you straighten yourself out and get a job, you bum?" I almost went for my gun to show the surly bastard I meant business.

"I *got* a job." He reached into his pants pocket, removed his wallet, and showed me his police badge. "I'm undercover on the strangler detail, you fucking clown. I'm staking out the area in case the killer shows up."

"No hard feelings." I tried to help him up, but he pushed my hand away. He got on his feet, put his wallet away, and pulled out his gun, which he pointed at me.

"You're under arrest for interfering with a police investigation."

"I'm a private detective. I was just trying to ask you a couple of questions."

"Also for assaulting a police officer."

"It's not my fault you got belligerent and took a swing at me. I was defending myself. How the hell was I supposed to know you're a cop? I mean your disguise is too authentic. You smell like a damn brewery. Who wouldn't believe you're a drunken slob?"

"Let's see some ID," he snarled. I showed him my investigator's license. He glanced at it. "Craven. Where have I heard that name before? I'm gonna run you downtown just for the hell of it."

"What if the strangler shows up while you're gone? They think he grabbed most of his victims in broad daylight."

"Why d'you think I'm here?"

"A neighbor thought you looked suspicious. That's why *I'm* here. Better put your gun away if you don't want to blow your cover. People are starting to come home from work." To make my point, an old Chrysler sedan pulled into the parking lot. He stuck the gun inside his jacket pocket.

"Get the fuck outta here," he said, trying to sound menacing.

"Hope you catch that madman before he strikes again," I said as I started to walk away. "If I were you, I wouldn't tangle with him. Just shoot him on sight."

TWENTY-THREE

The Wamsley Medical Center was an old three-story brown-brick structure with bars outside the windows on the top two floors. Using my map, I found the hospital on a country road just north of Glendale. I slammed the car door and tucked a clipboard under my arm. I left my gun and holster in the glove box.

It was early Tuesday morning. I yawned as I walked past a handful of cars in the parking lot and towards the building's main entrance. Wearing my brown suit—just back from the cleaners—and my new brown fedora, I was more than presentable. I pushed open the sturdy metal door and stepped into an empty lobby. Off to one side was a reception office and waiting room with an assortment of well-worn but unoccupied chairs. On the other side was an elevator. The arrow above the doors indicated the car was on the third floor. Maybe that's where everybody was. Straight ahead was a long green corridor with doors along both sides. The smell of disinfectant saturated the air like exhaust fumes from a backfiring truck.

About halfway down the hallway, a large gray-haired fellow was pushing a mop across the shiny linoleum floor. He was slowly headed in the other direction. At his pace, he might reach his destination sometime around nightfall. The big guy had on a green shirt, the kind worn in hospitals by staff or maybe patients. I couldn't remember. At any rate, this bozo wasn't wearing any pants. The hospital was a little chilly for such an oversight. Maybe he was a lazy orderly with a secret yearning for attention. Maybe he was a patient who liked to go sleepwalking with a mop. It wasn't my problem.

I stepped over to the reception window. The girl on duty had her arms folded on her desktop and her head resting on top of them. When I cleared my throat, she raised her head, yawned, and stretched. Looking around, she noticed me, pushed her hair back from her face, and got up. She smoothed out her white dress. I was hoping the sleepy girl, a pudgy brunette—probably only half an hour away from clocking out—would be more obliging than her wide-awake relief, who might show up at any minute. I figured a shift change was scheduled for eight.

"May I help you?" she asked as she approached the counter.

"Yes, ma'am, you certainly may. I'm Dudley O'Craven with MIME."

"*Who* are you with?"

"MIME. Maxwell Institute for Mental Education."

"Never heard of it," she said.

"We don't advertise. Look, we're conducting scientific research to coincide with our upcoming publicity campaign. It'll only take a minute of your time." I glanced at my watch and then poised a pencil over my clipboard. "I'd like to ask you some questions about one of your patients who underwent treatment here recently."

"Hold on a minute!" The receptionist stood rigidly behind the window. "If you don't advertise, how come you're doing a publicity campaign? Does that make any sense?"

"It does seem rather odd, now that you mention it."

"May I see some ID, Mr. O'Craven?" she asked sternly.

"Certainly," I said, placing my clipboard on the counter between us. I casually checked my pants pockets and then more hurriedly patted my suit coat, my jaw dropping as I made an effort to look alarmed. "I've been robbed! I bet it happened when I was in the lobby of my hotel. Some guy stumbled and fell against me as I was walking to the elevator. He had his hands all over me. I thought he was just trying to regain his balance, but he must've been going through my pockets. Son of a gun!" She looked at me in disbelief. "On the other hand," I added, "I may have left my wallet in my other suit when I changed clothes."

"Mr. O'Craven, just what *is* this research you're talking about?"

"MIME is gathering data on celebrities who've had mental health problems. It's all part of our Celebrity Mental Health Awareness Month. We want to spread the word that if famous people can seek help for mental problems, then that makes it okay for ordinary people—like you and me—to do likewise. We're trying to dispel the bugaboo about mental sickness. Most celebrities have undergone therapy of some kind at one time or another, and we intend to document and publicize their successful treatment. Now, I'd like to ask you about Simone Pearson's stay here."

The brunette looked at me thoughtfully and frowned. "Why? I wouldn't really call Miss Pearson's treatment a success. The newspapers said she killed herself in a car wreck."

"Exactly. She's the exception that proves the rule. Now could I please see her file?"

"I'll have to check with Dr. Wamsley. He should be in shortly."

"Look, I'm in a hurry," I said. "Do you realize just how many celebrities have spent time in mental wards in the Los Angeles area? I've been working on this project for a whole week, and I'm just getting started. Time is of the essence."

"Why do you need to see Miss Pearson's file?"

"I just want to verify the exact dates she was admitted and discharged." When she hesitated, I said, "Did I mention that I've been authorized by MIME to reward up to twenty dollars to anyone who is helpful in our important research?"

She turned and walked over to a row of filing cabinets, which—unlike the ones in my office—were probably jam-packed with paperwork. As she slid open a drawer, I thought I heard a scream coming from one of the floors above. Maybe it was just my imagination. Hospitals made me jittery. I reached for my pack of Chesterfields.

"Are you being helped?"

I spun around as an elderly gentleman, wearing a gray suit and carrying a briefcase, walked into the waiting room. The metal door closed quietly behind him.

"This nice young lady is taking care of me," I told him.

"I'm Dr. Wamsley." Pushing his thick glasses into place with a forefinger, he started walking my way. "Miss Brinker, what does this gentleman want?"

Miss Brinker was going through the file folders in one of the cabinet drawers and held up a finger. "Just a minute."

"Excuse me, Dr. Wamsley," I said. "I don't know the first thing about your hospital's dress policy. But if you look down the hall, I have a sneaking suspicion you'll find someone shamelessly disregarding it."

Squinting, he took a long look in the direction I was pointing. "Mr. Spangler, is that you?" he called down the corridor. "What in the world are you doing at this early hour? Aren't you taking your medication?" Wamsley glanced at me and hesitated for a moment. Then, shaking his head, he shuffled down the hall towards his errant patient. I turned to see the receptionist paging through a folder she'd placed on the counter.

"Where'd the doctor go?" she asked.

"He's checking on a disorderly patient. You all by yourself down here, Miss Brinker?"

"Everyone's upstairs handling a disturbance."

"That happen a lot?"

She didn't answer. "Let's see, Mr. O'Craven, I think the information you want is right here."

"May I take a look?" I reached out and turned Simone's file towards me. On a green form in the front of the file, the patient's date of admission was stamped 5/5/44, next to which was the almost legible signature of Dr. Wamsley. Below he'd scribbled the words "severe depression" and "drug addiction." I glanced down the page. The release date was stamped 5/18/44 and again signed with the same scrawl. Underneath was a scribbled note: "Send bill to Mr. V. McGahee. Beverly Hills Hotel."

I did some scribbling of my own on my clipboard. When I started to flip through the rest of the file, the receptionist grabbed the folder and closed it.

"What kind of treatment did Miss Pearson undergo?" I asked.

"I believe you've got what you came for." She held out her hand and I took out my wallet and gave her a ten. "Didn't you say your wallet was stolen?" she asked.

"Guess I was mistaken. What a relief."

"Anyway, you said there was a twenty-dollar reward."

"I said a reward of *up* to twenty dollars." I smiled pleasantly.

"Would you like me to summon Dr. Wamsley to settle this dispute?"

I quickly handed her another ten, picked up my clipboard, and turned to leave, almost bumping into a somber, gray-haired woman, perhaps Miss Brinker's replacement.

On the ride back to L.A., I tried to sort out some of what I'd learned. I had found the information Wesley Renfro wanted: a doctor's diagnosis of Simone's condition. In case of a lawsuit, Renfro's company, Uptowner, could get a court order for Simone's medical records. The doctor's opinion would bolster Uptowner's assertion that her death wasn't accidental. Vincent McGahee might not get his big payday after all. The V. McGahee who'd picked up the tab for Simone's hospital stay had to be the old man, Victor. Perhaps a talk with the oil tycoon himself was called for.

But first I decided to stop by the main library in downtown L.A. Browsing through old issues of the *Times*, I learned Vincent McGahee's airplane had been shot down May first, and he was subsequently hospitalized overseas. On the twenty-second, the war hero had been welcomed home in grand style at his Beverly Glen mansion. Celebrities, business leaders, and politicians alike had joined in the celebration. I could just imagine a bunch of fat cats whooping it up at the old man's expense.

So, Vincent's plane had been downed just days prior to Simone's admittance to the hospital, and she was released just before his return home. After their reunion, according to Vincent, he discovered Simone's problem with booze. Then Ashley was summoned to help her sister persevere. Back on the wagon, Simone landed her first movie role in months. When the wheels came off, I arrived on the scene to find out what happened to Simone, and I was still looking for clues. I left the library with a headache and an urge for a drink.

TWENTY-FOUR

Feeling as if I were stumbling around in the dark, I slouched in a comfortable armchair with my eyes closed, my head back, and a newspaper covering my face. I wondered what I was looking for, where to look for it, and who to ask about it. But I couldn't stop now. I had to keep searching, prying into other people's business, collecting clues—if that's what they were called. With enough information perhaps I could sort it out, put it together like a jigsaw puzzle, and then look for any missing pieces. I thought about the guy in the big red car. Was my life in some sort of danger? Under my suit coat, the .45 in my shoulder holster felt reassuring.

When I heard a ding, I opened my eyes and glanced sideways, around my newspaper, as the elevator doors parted. A beautiful young woman in a tight-fitting summer dress stepped out into the lobby. She paused and looked over her shoulder. An old gentleman with magnificent eyebrows and another man, husky and about forty, emerged and joined the woman. Both men wore dark-blue suits, but only the younger guy had a hat on. I handed my paper to one of the elderly idlers in my vicinity. Then I quickly crossed the lobby of the Beverly Hills Hotel. According to the clock on the wall, it was ten after twelve. After driving over from the public library, I'd waited maybe an hour in the luxury hotel for the old man to make an appearance. Minutes had crawled by like invisible fingers were holding back the hands of the clock. And now my patience had paid off.

"May I have a word with you, Mr. McGahee?" I asked, intercepting him before he could exit the building. "I'm a private detective investigating the death of your daughter-in-law." The burly guy shoved me out of the way as McGahee and the woman continued towards the exit.

"Handle this, Ant," McGahee ordered.

"I know Simone was being blackmailed," I said. Ant grabbed my wrist and twisted my arm behind my back.

"Hold on, Ant." McGahee had stopped and was now coming towards us. "Let's hear what this gentleman has to say." Others in the lobby were beginning to notice our lively discussion. Ant released my arm. McGahee turned back to the young woman. "Wait with Willie in the car, Sugar. I'll only be a minute."

Sugar nodded and departed as McGahee motioned Ant and me into the hotel's dimly lit lounge, where he found a corner booth away from the lunch crowd. While the old man waved off an approaching waiter, Ant smoothly reached inside my suit coat, took my gun from my shoulder holster, and shoved me into a seat. Sliding in beside me, he pocketed my Colt. McGahee nodded his approval and took the seat across from us. "You won't need your gun in here," he said. "Got a name?"

"Sidney Craven."

"Who do you work for, Mr. Cretin?"

"It's Craven, and I can't say, Mr. McGahee."

"Look, my time's valuable. My chauffeur is waiting out front in my limo. I'm already behind schedule. I'll give you exactly two minutes, starting now."

"This is that Dime Detective your son hired to find Simone," Ant said, poking a finger at me. "You can't trust him, Mr. McGahee. I wouldn't give—"

"Please, Ant, let him speak his piece." The old man looked at me. "You'll have to excuse my associate. Mr. Prior is only trying to protect my interests." McGahee motioned for me to continue.

"Thank you, sir. I hope your bodyguard's unwarranted interruption won't count against my time. By the way, Ant, do they call you Ant because you're such a big guy, you know, the way large guys are sometimes called Tiny?"

"It's short for Anthony," Ant said with a scowl.

"Thanks for clearing that up. Now, Mr. McGahee, your son discharged me right after Simone's body was identified. I'm presently working for a client who's concerned that your daughter-in-law's death might not have been an accident." The waiter returned with some menus but backed away when McGahee shook his head.

"I'm listening, Mr. Cretin," he said, rolling his beady eyes under those enormous brows.

"It's Craven. Did you know your daughter-in-law was being blackmailed?"

"What makes you think she was being blackmailed?"

"Mr. McGahee, let's not play games. I have less than two minutes. My guess is she went to you for the funds to pay the blackmailer. Where else would she get a large amount of money? I believe you wanted to avoid a scandal, so you came up with the hush money."

"Can you prove it?"

"Was the blackmailer continuing to harass your daughter-in-law?"

"Why would that matter to you, Mr. Cretin?"

"Well, Mr. McGa*hoo*, if the blackmailer was demanding more payments, it could lend credence to a theory I've been kicking around. I think Simone was worried your son might discover she was being blackmailed and then learn about her dirty little secret."

"What secret?"

"The secret she was being blackmailed over," I said, winking. "The stress may have unraveled her. She might have become upset enough to go on a bender and either purposely or recklessly drive off that canyon road."

"There's no good reason for you to go digging into my daughter-in-law's troubled past. My advice to you is let the deceased rest and spare the living any more sorrow."

"I'm just trying to learn the truth about Simone's death. I know she had mental health problems. You even paid the bill for her treatment. She was supposed to continue her career on the day she died. Something happened. I'm trying to find out what it was. And you're not helping."

"I think you've already found out enough."

"Perhaps too much," Ant added menacingly.

"Your time's up," McGahee said. "If you happen to be downtown at two o'clock, stop by city hall. I'm holding a news conference. It's open to the public. I'll be making an announcement you won't want to miss. You're a detective, right?"

"I've even got a license." I'd probably renew it one of these days.

"I'll show you how to catch a criminal. Now, if you'll excuse me, Mr. Cretin."

"If you'll tell your henchman to return my weapon, I'd appreciate it, Mr. McGa*hoo*." The old man ignored my request, got to his feet, and departed.

Ant dropped my gun on the floor. As I reached for it under the table, he hit me in the side of the neck with his fist. He mumbled something I couldn't really make out. I thought he said, "I took it for your own good." When I straightened up with my gun pointed in Ant's direction, he was gone.

My side was numb from the blow, but I decided to stick around. I knew the old man wouldn't volunteer anything. I just wanted him to more or less verify what I had already figured. He paid the blackmailer as well as the hospital. A couple more pieces of the puzzle.

I ordered the luncheon special from the waiter McGahee had shooed away earlier. I polished off an excellent seafood platter, downed a couple of drinks, and smoked a couple of cigarettes. When the waiter brought me the check, I had to look twice at the exorbitant amount. Well, it was Beverly Hills. I told the waiter to charge my lunch bill—along with a generous tip— to McGahee's account. After all, as I laughingly explained to the waiter, that's what wealthy friends are for.

I decided to take McGahee up on his invitation to city hall. I took Sunset into downtown, got stuck in traffic, made a number of turns, and then headed down Spring Street. I drove past the white building with the tall tower and double-parked alongside a black Caddie. It was shortly after two when I climbed the countless steps that led to the rotunda with its high arches and colorful tile floor. A crowd of about three hundred was gathered around a makeshift platform where McGahee, Mayor Roy Gundy, and two uniformed cops were standing. The mayor had just introduced the oil tycoon, who stepped forward and got a round of polite applause.

"Thank you, Mayor Gundy, for that wonderful introduction," McGahee said. "Ladies and gentlemen, I don't believe in small talk, so let me get straight to the point. Today, I'm announcing a fifty-thousand-dollar reward for anyone who comes forward with information leading to the capture and conviction of the so-called Starlet Strangler." Cheers went up from the crowd. "We've got to put a stop to this killing spree. Our city's good name is being tarnished by some lunatic. We simply can't allow this terror to continue. My friends, I predict the police will make an arrest by the end of the week."

As the crowd applauded, a newspaper reporter standing near the platform identified himself and called out a question. "Ben Luper with the *Times*. How can you be so sure the police will nab the strangler in the next few days? He's been on the loose for five weeks now."

"My generous offer will provide the incentive our good citizens need," McGahee explained. "Now, everyone will be on the lookout for this madman. Greed is a great motivator. We'll get him."

"Why did you wait so long to offer a reward?" Luper asked.

"There's no time like the present," McGahee responded, smiling broadly.

"Brenley with the *Mirror*." Fat Bert sounded like he was way up front. "You seem so sure of yourself, Mr. McGahee. Would you be willing to double your reward if the strangler isn't caught by Saturday?"

McGahee raised and lowered his brows, obviously milking the moment. "I'll spend whatever money it takes to save lives. You can count on me just like my investors do. I've bankrolled any number of worthy causes in my lifetime." The phony bastard was more interested in promoting his business than in catching the strangler.

"Is the fifty grand your own money?" I shouted from the back. "Or is it money you've swindled from your investors?" There was a murmur in the gathering as heads turned in my direction.

"I didn't catch your name," McGahee said.

"Cretin," I replied. "I'm with the *Daily Sham*."

"I could have you arrested for slander," he said angrily.

The mayor quickly stepped forward. "Thank you all for coming out today," he said, recapturing the crowd's attention. "And thank *you*, Mr. McGahee, for your help in fighting crime in the City of Angels." That must have been a cue for one of the cops. He hoisted a gigantic cardboard rectangle and handed it over to McGahee. It was an oversized check made out for fifty grand in large writing visible to everyone. With Gundy's help, the old man held up the piece of cardboard. Flashbulbs popped as photographers moved in for close-ups of the two smiling friends.

When the crowd started clapping again, I made my way out. Going down the steps, I noticed a cop writing parking tickets. I reached my Ford just before he did.

"You're illegally parked," the cop said. "And you better get your window fixed. You're lucky I reached my quota of tickets for the month." He took a close look at my sedan. "What'd you do, roll it?"

"Yeah, but I'll be driving a brand-new automobile when I get that big reward." I laughed. When the cop looked puzzled, I said, "Victor McGahee just offered fifty grand to anyone who turns in the Starlet Strangler."

"So that's what all the hoopla's about," he said with a nod towards city hall. "That millionaire banker's gonna cause us a big headache."

"Don't you think the reward's a good idea?"

"The phones won't stop ringing, and we'll be chasing down bogus tips from every crackpot in the city. It's a publicity stunt. If the killer gets caught, McGahee will claim all the credit."

"Life just isn't fair." I got into my Ford and glanced back at city hall. Ant was standing at the top of the steps, his arms folded across his chest. I couldn't be sure, but it looked as if he was scowling. People were starting to exit the building. I waved to the cop as I drove off.

TWENTY-FIVE

During a band break at the Red-Hot Charcoal on Tuesday night, I informed Nehemiah in some detail about how Simone had become a blackmail victim. We were both standing at the bar. I told him Bert Brenley had somehow obtained a photo of the couple.

"Her father-in-law came up with the extortion money for Brenley *and* picked up the bill for her stay in the hospital," I said. "But I don't think her husband ever found out. He never said a word about any of it to me. My guess is the old man never told his son. He's a banker. A scandal would be bad for business."

"Simone never told me about any shakedown." Nehemiah pounded his fist on the bar next to my drink, and some of the whiskey sloshed over the side of my glass. "I remember now. The two of us were just standing outside the Charcoal about closing time. Some fat white dude jumps out of his car, runs over with his camera and snaps a photo. Scares the hell out of us when the flashbulb goes off. Then he jumps back in his car and drives away. Simone got upset, but I just laughed it off. Figured it was some dopey tourist taking a photo. Maybe he never saw a mixed couple before."

"That was Brenley. He must've tailed her to the Charcoal from her house. That's the photo he used to blackmail Simone."

"Too bad I didn't know what the fuck was going on," he said heatedly. "That's around the time our romance hit the skids, and she started her daytime drinking. It figures. I'd of taken care of that reporter."

"What could you have done?"

Nehemiah smiled grimly. "Let's see, Simone pays off this tabloid blackmailer, and she's getting back into movies when all of a sudden she swipes some fancy clothes and then wrecks her car." There was more than a hint of cynicism in his voice.

"Relapses happen," I said. "Maybe Brenley was still blackmailing her. Those bastards can be persistent. If her affair with you and her abortion ever made it into the newspapers, her marriage and her life of luxury would most likely have been over. Don't forget that her film career was already in limbo. Simone must have just come undone. The coroner's report said she'd been drinking prior to her death."

"No way Simone killed herself," he said. "She just wasn't a quitter."

"It could have been an accident." I downed my whiskey and then lit a cigarette.

"Or maybe she told this asshole Brenley to go to hell and they got into an argument."

"And she slapped him and kicked him," I said, "and then *he* got really mad and broke her neck. Then what? How'd he get her car *and* her body to the bottom of that canyon?"

Nehemiah shook his head and frowned. Then he reached for his wallet. Despite my protests, admittedly feeble, he forced two fifties on me. As I pocketed the money, I told him about my adventure on Topanga Canyon.

"Maybe you're getting close and somebody's getting nervous," he said thoughtfully. "I want you to keep searching, Sidney. I got a feeling there's a lot more to be uncovered." He motioned for the bartender. "Drinks are on the house for my friend."

The bartender nodded, and I pushed away my empty glass and ordered a double whiskey. Nehemiah rejoined the other band members, now back from their break. For some reason, I didn't have my usual craving for alcohol. I barely listened to the music as I nursed my drink. The joint was hopping, and the crowd noise was giving me a headache. My investigation had stalled. I didn't know where to turn. Now that I had Nehemiah's cash, however, I was obliged to sniff around for more clues.

Shortly after the band's set ended, I hit the john. The stench of urine didn't quite mask the smell of reefer smoke in the air. Making my exit, I was happy to see my Ford across the street from the Charcoal—exactly where

I'd left it. Stanley, in a black suit and derby, had been out front when I arrived. The bouncer had given me a nasty look but allowed me to enter the club. He was gone now. When I got into my car and shut the door, I found Loretta sitting on the passenger side. She had on a short, glittery dress that exposed most of her shapely legs. I almost didn't notice her large purple earrings and matching lipstick.

"Don't get excited and pull out your gun," the Sweet Delight said quickly.

"Why would I, Loretta?" I raised my eyebrows.

"You did last week when I was sitting in here with Jerome."

"As long as you don't try to steal my wheels, you got nothing to worry about," I said, smiling reassuringly. "By the way, where *is* your boyfriend?"

"Don't worry about him. He drove off somewhere with Stanley. You left your door unlocked, peeper. When you're that careless, you never know who you might find in your automobile."

"Since I rolled it, the lock on the driver's door doesn't work anymore, and the other door won't even open."

"Yeah, I noticed your car's sort of rough looking."

"Let me guess, Loretta. You've got something you want to tell me about Simone Pearson."

"How'd you know?"

"Just a hunch."

"How much would you pay for what I know about that little whore?"

"Depends on what you know."

"I know Nehemiah gave you a wad of dough to snoop around. That SOB pays me peanuts to sing my heart out every night. I figure he owes me. And this is as good a way as any to collect. Now, do we got a deal?" I took a twenty from my wallet and—keeping it out of Loretta's reach—showed it to her. She smiled, displaying a gold tooth that glittered like a headlight. "Did you know Simone was being blackmailed?"

I nodded.

"Did you know who the creep was?"

"Of course," I said condescendingly. "I'm a detective."

"Did you know some other creep raped her?"

"What?"

"That's right, big boy. One guy wanted money, and the other guy wanted sex. Hey, whatever gets you through the night." She reached for the bill, but I shook my head.

"Not until I hear everything you know." I cranked down my window. I was hoping some fresh air would neutralize the strong scent of her perfume.

"The world is full of tightwads." Loretta sighed wearily. I offered her a Chesterfield, took one for myself, and lit a match on my thumbnail. As we sat in a smoky haze, she said, "Simone confided in me one night a few months ago. It was before I became a Delight, when I just used to hang out at the Charcoal. I had just gave her a fix in the back room. You know, she was about the same age as me. And I was a user myself, but I kicked the habit."

I nodded as I looked at the needle tracks on her arm.

"Simone was as low as I ever seen her," Loretta continued. "She starts to unwind and tells me about how she comes to be blackmailed on account of Nehemiah getting her knocked up. Some news reporter gets the lowdown on what she done. And a Hollywood tabloid's gonna run the story and ruin her movie career if she don't pay up. I didn't even know the floozy was an actress. So she goes to her father-in-law, some filthy-rich oil tycoon. Man's stingy as hell when it comes to his family. He thinks about it for a while, and then he sends some gangster what works for him over to Simone's house with the shakedown money." Loretta glanced out the window at two young guys in baggy suits and black derbies. They had just walked up to the car.

"Hey, Lo, everything all right?" one asked. He bent down and looked in the driver's window.

"I ain't studying you, Slick," Loretta told him.

"Got a smoke, man?" he asked, looking at me. When I got out my pack, Loretta pushed my hand away. She took a drag from her cigarette, reached past me, and handed it to him.

"How'm I supposed to smoke that cigarette? It don't got any flavor," Loretta complained. "It's like eating candy without taking off the wrapper."

The two guys laughed. Slick took a drag from the Chesterfield, which had a purple lipstick smudge on it. "Tastes just fine," he said as he exhaled a cloud of smoke.

"Get your feet off the street," Loretta said. "I got business with this gentleman. Maybe I'll let you buy me a shot later—if Jerome ain't around." The two guys drifted back towards the club.

"Who raped Simone?" I asked.

"I'm getting to that part. The gangster what brings over the hush money forces himself on Simone. She finally gets away from the guy, but she's hysterical. She runs outta the house and hides behind some bushes in the backyard until he takes off. When she goes back in the house, she looks all over for the shakedown money. She finds it floating in the toilet bowl. The motherfucker pissed on the money. Simone fishes it out and counts it. Money's all there, but now she's afraid of this hoodlum coming back."

"Did she tell you the guy's name?"

Loretta shook her head.

"I know who he is. The old man's bodyguard." I threw my cigarette butt out the window. "They don't come much sleazier."

"Anyway, Simone asks Nehemiah to get her a gun. Makes up some phony excuse. She don't wanna tell him what's really going on. She don't want him getting mixed up in it. Just wants a gun so she can hold off the gangster if he ever tries something again." Loretta laughed and leaned into me with her ample bosom. She snatched the twenty from my grasp.

"That's all I know," she said. "Ain't told nobody. Not even Nehemiah. Just you, sweetie. Getting blackmailed and then what that gangster done really messed up Simone. I know that's about when she started using the hard stuff. Before then she just drank and smoked reefers. But I guess she got herself cured. She was gonna make a movie. I saw a story about her in one of them tabloids Nehemiah's always reading. They got all sorts of gossip about movie stars. Think they make up half the stuff. Problem is you can't tell what half. I don't pay no attention to 'em. Guess Nehemiah was trying to keep track of what was going on with Simone. It's funny. I used to think she was just a lousy nightclub singer."

"You didn't like her much, did you?"

"I felt sorry for her until she started sleeping with everybody at the Charcoal."

"Even Jerome?"

"He's lucky I didn't catch his black ass."

"You're still mad about it, aren't you?"

"You know," she said sadly, "Nehemiah tried to look out for her, but she was a white girl. That's risky for a black man." She looked at her watch. "My break is over. If I'm late Nehemiah's gonna dock me." Loretta tried her door and when it didn't open, she slid over in my direction. I got out and she followed. "See you around, peeper." Provocatively shaking her ass, she strolled towards the Charcoal.

TWENTY-SIX

I was feeling restless and decided on taking a detour before heading home. I took Central to Olympic, drove west to Beverly Glen, and then north, right past the McGahee mansion. The lights were off and the war hero's black Buick was parked in the driveway. Even the wealthy needed sleep. I turned east onto Mulholland Drive and continued on that long, winding road all the way to Laurel Canyon Boulevard. My head was crowded with thoughts—like hornets in a nest—as I turned south and headed back to the city. I wasn't too preoccupied, however, to notice that a red Lincoln had been in my rearview mirror since I left the Charcoal. It looked like the same car that tailed me last week. Maybe it was also the car that forced me off the road on Topanga Canyon.

Turning east onto Sunset, I headed for Alvarado. I lost the tail by changing lanes and running a red light. Minutes later I spotted the Lincoln two cars ahead of me. I wasn't in the mood for games. I took a number of side streets as I headed for my apartment building. By the time I pulled into my parking lot, the Lincoln was long gone.

Once in my apartment, I switched on the lights and then the radio. I loosened my tie and settled into my easy chair. It had been an exhausting day. I was too tired to remove my suit coat or kick off my shoes. Just as I closed my eyes and started to relax, someone knocked on my door. I waited and the knocking resumed—more urgently this time. As I walked over to the door, I took off my fedora and flung it on the couch.

"Who is it?"

"Got some important news about Simone Pearson," someone said in a muffled voice. When I unlocked and opened the door, Ant roughly pushed me back inside my apartment. He followed me in and slammed the door. I quickly drew my gun from my shoulder holster, but Ant slapped it away, and it clattered onto the floor.

"What the hell?" I said. "You can't just come barging in here."

"Shut up and sit down, Craven."

I glanced longingly at my weapon on the floor and then looked at Ant who was pointing his own gun—a snub-nosed .38 revolver—at my heart. I decided to sit down in my chair and shut up. He picked up my gun and stashed it in his coat pocket for the second time today.

"If I ever want a backup firearm, I know just the person to see." He was laughing as he walked over to the couch and sat down on my fedora—my new fedora. But I had more serious problems at the moment. A gangster with two guns was in my apartment. My living room was small, and now it seemed as crowded as a trendy nightspot on a Saturday night. "Didn't you notice me tailing you, peeper?"

"That was *you* in the Lincoln. I tried to shake you." I paused, then started yelling. "You son of a bitch! You were the one who ran me off the road. You tried to kill me. My girl was in the car."

"It was just a warning," he said nonchalantly. "I was tooling along Coast Highway when I saw you turn onto Topanga Canyon. I took advantage of the situation. Just having some fun. If I wanted to kill you, we wouldn't be talking now."

"I thought you might be a drunken driver."

"Guess you rolled your heap when I blew past you. I like the new look. It fits your shabby style." Ant laughed. "Ever have any problem with your fan belt?"

"Don't tell me, but that was another warning, right?"

He laughed again.

"I figured it was just a faulty fan belt," I said. "Why didn't you tamper with my brakes? Isn't that what gangsters do in the movies? I got a better idea. Next time you want to send me a message, leave a note under my wiper blade. Just spell it out so there's no doubt. Hey, that's a rhyme. Should be easy for you to remember. What's the point in scaring the hell out of me if you don't tell me what's going on?"

"For a detective you're a joke. I gave you a clue about your fan belt when I returned your gun at the hotel. I told you to look under your hood."

"What? I thought you told me you took it for my own good. I assumed you were talking about my gun. I figured maybe you were worried I might accidentally shoot myself."

"Don't play dumb, peeper. Now, did you think showing up at city hall was a smart move?"

"I got a personal invitation from the old man. You're saying he wasn't glad to see me?"

"Believe it or not, the old man was annoyed with your crack about him swindling investors." He was gesturing with his hands, and his gun was pointed at the ceiling. Now he aimed it in my direction. "The old man don't want you nosing around in his business *or* his family's business. He can't sleep nights because of you."

"He worries too much," I said, trying to sound concerned. "He'll get ulcers."

"He's already got 'em," he growled. "Okay, smart guy, we need to talk."

"Don't tell me your boss has decided to cooperate with my investigation. Did my earlier questioning soften him up? Is he ready to come clean?"

"Here's the question. How much do you know about Simone's bad behavior?"

"Mind if I smoke?"

"Answer the question."

"I just know she was being blackmailed." I gave him a lopsided grin.

"Wrong answer, snooper. When I read in the *Mirror* you were working for Simone's hubby, naturally I wanted to see what you were up to."

"Naturally."

"I couldn't believe Vincent would hire you. I mean, you accuse his wife of shoplifting, and then she kicks the shit out of you. Who cares what really happened? This city's crawling with private eyes. And he picks you. He don't even tell the old man Simone disappeared or that he hired a snooper to find her. I had to break the news to him. Want to know how I found you?"

"Not especially," I said with a yawn.

Ant pushed his hat back from his forehead with the barrel of his gun and frowned. "I was waiting for you in the lobby of your office building about a week ago when you got off the elevator. You were working late. I recognized you from the tabloid photo. I tailed you to that colored joint on Central. That's the night I cut your fan belt. You parked in the perfect spot. It was nice and dark." As he bragged about his prank, I tried to think of a way to disarm him. But I figured any move on my part would lead to only one outcome: my sudden death.

"And you went back to the same joint again tonight," he said gruffly. "What the hell you been doing?"

"A black guy bought my car last week. He even took it for a test drive. But then he had a change of heart. Guess you didn't hang around after you fixed my fan belt. You missed our business transaction."

"*Nobody* would even *think* about buying your heap, even before you rolled it. Come on. You can do better than that."

"Okay, I happen to like red-hot jazz. They got these two sexy colored girls that just knock me out with the way they swing and sway. They're a classy act. Since you're a bigot, you wouldn't appreciate it."

Ant jumped off the couch and jabbed his gun against my temple. "No more bullshit! Or I'll blow a hole in your fucking head big enough to put my fist through." He walked over and turned up the radio, which was full of static. "That should muffle a gunshot. Besides, in this neighborhood nobody cares if you shoot off a gun as long as you're not aiming at *them*." Laughing, he turned down the volume and reduced the static by tuning in the station. "We got some background music. Now, talk!" His gun was inches from my head as he stood over me.

"I forgot the question."

His gun roughly probed my ear.

"Oh, yeah. About Simone. I found out she got pregnant and had an abortion," I croaked. "Your boss came up with the hush money for the blackmailer."

"Who was blackmailing her?"

"How the hell should I know? I'm only a dime detective."

He whacked the side of my head with his gun.

"Damn! That fucking hurts!" I covered up with my hands.

"Maybe I should turn up the radio and end our conversation right now."

"Bert Brenley," I said, turning away.

"That slimy reporter with the *Mirror?* The *nerve* of that bastard." His show of surprise was as phony as a hooker's smile. I got the feeling he knew all along. He lowered his weapon.

"Yeah, what a son of a bitch." I looked scornfully at the gunman.

"You know how the cash got doled out?"

"The old man handed out the money to you," I said, keeping my eye on his gun. "And you delivered it to Simone. Somehow Brenley got it from her."

"How'd you find out?"

"A colored girl from the Charcoal told me tonight." I winced as I gingerly felt the knot on my head.

"The two of you were getting kinda cozy in your car. I was parked up the street. I didn't think she was ever gonna leave. Tell me what you found out about me." His gun was at my temple again.

"Don't shoot!" I slumped back in the chair. "You raped Simone." The thought made me grimace. He lowered his gun and stepped back.

"She was sleeping with a nigger trumpet player," he said with a smirk. "But she didn't think *I* was good enough for her. She told old man McGahee she was stepping out with one of her costars. He thinks some actor knocked her up and paid for the abortion. If he found out the truth, he'd of strangled her with his own hands. Everyone knows the old guy struck it rich in Texas. What his righteous high-society cronies here in L.A. *don't* know is he used to belong to the KKK. He might of left his Klan hood and white sheet in Texas but not his hate for Negroes."

"Sounds like your boss is one hell of a compassionate guy."

"You don't have a clue. Victor went out of his way to help that tramp. She was a damn junkie. She was all screwed up. When Simone got the news that her husband's plane was shot down and he was coming home from overseas, she had a nervous breakdown."

"With all the crap she'd been through," I said, "that was probably the last straw."

"She got arrested for driving the wrong way on a one-way street. She was higher than a kite. The cops called Victor, and he picked her up from the station. As a favor to the old man, they didn't book her. Next day I found her sitting in her Packard in her driveway, trying to start the car with her house key. She was in a fucking daze. Victor had her quietly committed to a hospital in Glendale. They got her off drugs. They gave her electroshock therapy. That's a brand-new procedure and it cost him a bundle. Getting zapped with all them damn volts probably scared the hell out of her. But it worked, because she acted different afterwards. She wasn't so headstrong anymore. She was easier for the old man to manage."

Ant laughed and shook his head. "Victor didn't want nobody finding out she was in a loony bin. He wanted a phony story the two of them could use on his son and anyone else who wondered about Simone's recovery. You know, because everyone heard rumors about her drinking habit. So he took her to one of them loopy revival meetings with Sister Aimee. And what do you know? God worked wonders, and suddenly Simone's on the wagon. Anyway, that's how they planned to explain her big transformation. And everyone bought it. The old man wanted her marriage to work out."

"He wanted to avoid any whiff of scandal," I said. "Who knows what the tabloids might discover about him and his family once they start sniffing around? I can see the headline: KLAN BANKER PAYS BLACKMAILER WITH SWINDLED MONEY."

"You're just a barrel of laughs. Who the hell you been working for?" he said with a snarl.

"Thought you'd never ask. But I can't tell you. You probably don't know that private eyes like me follow a code of conduct. Our clients have the right to remain anonymous."

He quickly raised his gun.

"Uptowner Life," I said. At least I could keep Nehemiah's name out of it. Ant would never suspect I had two clients.

"Why'd an insurance company wanna hire a crummy snooper like you?"

"They're on the hook for a substantial sum because of Simone's car crash. Vincent's the beneficiary."

"That damn millionaire's son needs money like you need a hole in the head."

"You'll be glad to know Uptowner hired me to see that his payday never comes."

"All I know is they're gonna need a replacement. They probably been paying you next to nothing. And all the hassles you been going through. You gotta ask yourself one question. Was it worth it?" He hooted. "Ready for one last ride, Dime Detective?"

"Huh?"

"You know too much. You should of laid off the case. The old man warned you to stop your snooping."

"I thought he was just giving me some friendly advice. I didn't take it as a death threat."

"Sometimes you gotta read between the lines. I already gave you a couple warnings."

"Those warnings shouldn't count. I mean, I hadn't even talked to you or the old man yet. How could I possibly figure it out? Look, now that you've explained it to me, maybe we can work something out."

"No second chances with the old man," he said coldly. "When his wife wanted him out of her life, he refused to give her a divorce. He didn't wanna pay her all that alimony she wanted. It would of ended up in court with her blabbing everything she knew about his wheeling and dealing—which was plenty. But she kinda got what she wanted anyway. She was found dead from an overdose of sleeping pills. No messy divorce, but she got him out of her life." He laughed harshly. "Just like her, you could cause trouble if you ever decided to talk to the cops or the press."

"Who would believe me anyway?" I tried to sound convincing. "I won't talk. You can trust me."

"Save your breath. Your word don't mean shit to me. Nobody can trust nobody. Take the old man. He don't trust me, and I don't trust him. We both got the goods on each other. That way he'll think twice before giving me up to save his own ass and vice versa. For me, it's kinda like job insurance."

"Who's gonna take *your* word against his?"

"Don't worry, I got everything in writing, and I keep it handy," he said boastfully. "Now, on your feet, snooper." I slowly stood up. He plucked my misshapen hat off the couch and jammed it crookedly on my head. He'd kept *his* hat on the whole time. "We're going for a spin in my Lincoln. I think you'll find it a superior ride when compared to your clunker."

TWENTY-SEVEN

Ant was right. His Lincoln *was* a luxury ride. I drove while he leaned back in the corner on the passenger side, his gun pointed my way. At his insistence, I drove down Sunset, turned north onto Laurel Canyon, and then west onto Mulholland. We were driving the same route I had taken earlier when he was tailing me. Only now we were traveling in the opposite direction. Light rain began falling, and I turned on the windshield wipers. We rode in silence. The only sound came from the lazy motion of the wipers.

"Slow down and pull over," Ant said, sticking his gun in my side. I pulled over and parked at an angle on a turnout between the road and the edge of a deep canyon. We were on a forlorn part of Mulholland that overlooked the San Fernando Valley. "I thought you might appreciate this excellent vista."

"Very considerate of you, Ant. But we've already seen this view tonight. Don't you remember? We both drove by earlier in separate cars. Say, why don't we go to Griffith Observatory and look at the stars?"

"It's too cloudy, asshole," he barked.

"Okay, then we could—"

"All right, Craven, out of the car." When he motioned with his gun, I turned off the motor and opened the door. He moved over and then exited on the driver's side, right behind me. "Try to run and you're a dead man."

"And if I don't run?"

He ignored my question, jammed his gun in my back, and prodded me towards the brink of the canyon. Down below, the lights in the Valley sparkled like a starry night in the country. The sky above, however, was dark with storm clouds that had gathered after nightfall. A passing car, its tires making a hissing noise on the wet road, momentarily lit up our little scene. The driver may have assumed we were sightseers. Just a couple of jokers standing near the edge of a cliff on a rainy and windy night.

Safe in their brightly lit houses below, ordinary people were reading their newspapers and listening to their radios. They were doing ordinary things. I wanted to do ordinary things. But I had a feeling Ant had other ideas.

"You know, that snobby Pearson bitch used to strut around like she had the world on a string," he said, apparently in the mood for reminiscing. "For a small-time actress, she had a big-time attitude. Never treated me with any respect when she saw me with the old man. And I'm his business associate."

"Is that what you call it?"

"Look who she takes up with," he said, disregarding my comment. "And her husband stationed overseas. She'd be gone for days sometimes. I know because I kept watch on the Beverly Glen mansion. She was nothing but a whore." He paused in his tirade.

"But she wouldn't sleep with *you*. So you forced yourself on her."

"I was drunk. Anyhow, she had it coming for all the times she snubbed me. I just wanted her to show me some appreciation for bringing over the hush money. Next time I dropped by with the cash, Simone lets me in the house like everything's okay. I figured she'd let bygones be bygones. But she's got this faraway look in her eyes. I could tell she was hopped up. The crazy broad pulls a gun on me and takes a potshot at me. Lucky her aim was off. She hits one of them expensive paintings they got hanging on the wall. I just threw the money at her and got the hell outta there. After that, she won't even open the door for me. Makes me leave the money in the mailbox. You know, I could of told the old man who she was really shacked up with. But I was trying to look after her, and she acts like she don't trust me. That's what I mean about her not showing me no respect." He snorted loudly.

"Excuse me, but shouldn't we get out of the rain?" I said. "We could catch pneumonia." He ignored my suggestion and shoved me forward.

"It's only fitting that the detective who couldn't find Simone ends up at the bottom of a canyon just like she did," Ant said. "Isn't that what they call *irony*?" He laughed. I tried to swallow but my throat was too dry.

"It'd be more ironic if *you* wound up down there," I said hoarsely as I glanced over the rim of the canyon.

"What?"

"I thought Simone's death might have been an accident, but you killed her, didn't you? Just like with his wife, the old guy couldn't trust Simone. He was afraid she might go haywire and maybe go to the cops about the fix she was in. The press would have been all over the story."

"Maybe the old man's not the only one who had a motive," Ant said mockingly. "You should of sniffed around Beverly Glen." He paused when a car sped into view, skidded off the road, and came to a stop on the other side of the red Lincoln. The headlights went out. Two doors opened and slammed shut, and a couple of crouching figures approached Ant's car. Ant pointed his gun in their direction. "What the hell you guys want?" When they arrived at the Lincoln, they stayed in the shadows. One creeping to the front of the car and the other to the rear, they took cover behind the big vehicle about twenty feet from us.

"Don't fuck with me!" Ant yelled, firing a shot over their heads. "Or I'll blast your asses off!"

"Who you trying to fool?" someone shouted in a familiar voice. "Out there in the open, you gotta be about the easiest target I ever seen!"

When a car loaded with shouting and laughing revelers roared by, its headlights revealed the two men hunched down behind Ant's vehicle. Despite my run-in with them at the Red-Hot Charcoal, I was somehow heartened to see Stanley and Jerome. Then I noticed they were both holding guns at arm's length and pointing them our way. I started edging away from Ant until I felt the barrel of his gun in my back.

"Ain't you boys outta your neighborhood?" Ant said. "Better hit the road while you still can!"

"Play it smart and throw down your weapon!" Stanley countered. "If you had any sense, you'd be crapping your pants about now!"

"This is your last chance to save your black butts!" Ant hooked one arm around my neck and pulled me backwards with him. Resting his other arm on my shoulder, he aimed his gun at the intruders.

"Don't use the peeper for a shield!" Stanley said. "Let him go, and shoot it out like a man!"

I'd heard enough tough-guy banter for one night. I rammed my elbow into Ant's stomach. He groaned and loosened his hold on me. Then I turned around and punched him in the face. I heard a crunching sound as his nose bent sideways. He lost his balance on the slippery ground but grabbed onto my coat, and we both fell down. Our hats went flying when we tumbled and rolled around close to the canyon's edge. I was on top of him and then under him as I tried to wrench the gun from his grasp. When I finally let go of his weapon, he rolled off me, and I scrambled away.

Ant fired two shots in my direction, but the bullets whizzed by my head and slammed into the ground. My ears were ringing, and my heart was pounding like a jackhammer ripping up concrete. Then Stanley and Jerome opened fire. Ant, who was hunkered down, traded shots with them. Flattening myself against the ground, I flinched every time I saw a muzzle flash.

Suddenly the gangster howled in pain and began shouting obscenities. He rolled onto his side and fumbled with his revolver as he tried to feed more cartridges into the cylinder. I considered creeping up on Ant while he was busy reloading, but then he reached into the coat pocket where he'd put *my* gun. In an apparent show of bravado, Ant regained his footing and—with a weapon in each hand—began shooting wildly at the two Negroes. I heard the sounds of glass breaking and metal puncturing as his bullets struck his own vehicle.

With bullets once again flying in both directions, Ant began staggering about aimlessly. Defiantly waving both guns in the air, he stumbled backwards over the precipice and disappeared into the darkness below.

TWENTY-EIGHT

While Jerome and Stanley stood over me, I tried to calm down and breathe normally. Jerome extended an arm and helped me to my feet. "What're you two doing here?" I asked as I started looking around in the darkness.

"Nehemiah wanted us to follow you," Stanley said. He took out a small flashlight from his suit coat. "Lose something?" When he played the light over the area where I'd grappled with the gangster, I glimpsed two hats on the ground nearby. I walked over, picked up mine, and spitefully kicked Ant's fedora into the canyon.

"He forgot his hat." I looked over at Stanley. "Are you saying Nehemiah's worried about me?"

"Hell, no," Jerome answered. "He wants us to make sure you're doing your job, you know, earning all that money he's paying you."

"So you're saying he doesn't trust me? Then, why'd he hire me in the first place?"

"Search me."

I put on my hat and started to brush off my clothes. Stanley turned his flashlight on me. "You didn't take a bullet, did you?" he asked. My shirt and suit coat were streaked with blood.

I shook my head. "I think I broke his nose, and the bastard bled all over me when we were rolling around over here." The knuckles on my right hand were swollen, but my fingers worked okay. We walked on the turnout over to the two parked cars. We stopped beside Ant's vehicle, and Stanley shined his flashlight on it.

"What we gonna do about tough guy's Lincoln?" Jerome asked.

"The dumb bastard shot the shit out of his own automobile," Stanley said, laughing. The windshield had taken a number of hits, and both headlights were shot out. The car was riddled with bullet holes.

"Hey, the keys are in it," Jerome said. "A little body work and a new coat of paint, and it'll be good as new."

"Cops catch Negroes riding in this high-priced vehicle," Stanley said, "they gonna figure we stole it and pull us over. Then they got us for murder. We ain't taking no chances." He opened the driver's door and lit up the car's interior with his flashlight. He reached over and rummaged through the glove box. Stanley removed a pair of gloves, a map, and a large manila envelope. Killing the light, he stuffed everything into his pockets and then shifted the clutch into neutral. "Come on, peeper, give us a hand. You and Jerome push from the rear end."

With all of us grunting loudly, we somehow managed to roll the heavy car to the edge of the cliff. There was no guardrail to hamper our progress. Once moving, the car's own momentum carried it over the side and out of sight. We heard it bouncing and crashing on its journey downward. Then it stopped. No explosion. No flames lighting up the night sky. Nothing dramatic. Just silence. Then we heard a car approaching. Tires squealing, it sped around the bend and was quickly gone.

"The cops ought to have fun trying to figure this one out," Jerome said. Lightning flashed overhead as we walked towards their vehicle, a Plymouth sedan that looked like it had a brand-new paint job.

"Can we drop *you* somewhere?" Stanley asked with a laugh. He climbed under the wheel, Jerome joined him in the front seat, and I got in back.

"My apartment on Alvarado would be nice. Just take—"

"I already know," Stanley said. "We been following you all over the place tonight. We were parked around the corner from the Charcoal when you drove by. Didn't take us long to figure out we weren't the only ones tailing you. Then we waited forever in the parking lot for you and tough guy to come back outta that rat hole you live in. By the way, who *was* that stupid shit? Even with two guns, he couldn't shoot straight."

"Old man McGahee's right-hand man, bodyguard, henchman," I said. "Take your pick."

"Old man *who?*" he asked.

"Victor McGahee, the oil tycoon. He was Simone Pearson's father-in-law."

"Never heard of him," Stanley said. "Ride home's gonna cost you." Casually turning around, he aimed the long barrel of a .45 revolver at me. "Hand over the hundred bucks you owe me."

"I don't owe you a hundred bucks. Besides, I don't have that much money."

"Don't give me no bullshit, snooper. Nehemiah paid you tonight. Fork it over or I'll bust a cap in your ass and make you walk home in the rain." A sudden downpour began hammering the roof of the car and splashing against the windows.

"If anything, I only owe you fifty. Of the hundred I took off you, I gave Jerome half to get my car back."

"Say what?" Jerome said. "That was my money to start with."

Stanley looked over at Jerome. "You got a point, my man, but only forty of it was yours. What you paid me for the snooper's car."

"But I sold it back to him for fifty," his partner said. "Hell, a man's got a right to make a profit on a business transaction, don't he?"

"The other ten's mine, Jerome. It was part of *my* money what white boy here stole from my wallet." He held out his hand, and Jerome reluctantly pulled out a large roll, peeled off a ten, and gave it to Stanley. "Okay, now I'll take the fifty *you* owe me, snooper, and another twenty for medical expenses, and then we'll call it even." Stanley lifted his hat to give me a close-up look at his blood-stained bandage. "If you wasn't working for my boss, you wouldn't be sitting in my car right now. Wanna take a guess where you'd be?"

"Did Nehemiah really send you guys to tail me?"

"Yeah, but that don't mean we can't take care of some side business while we're at it," Stanley said.

Too tired to protest any longer, I gave Stanley a fifty from my wallet. "I can't keep track of what belongs to who and who paid what to who and why they paid it." When he kept holding out his hand, I reluctantly took out a twenty. "How about this?" I said. "Give me the envelope from the gangster's glove box, and I'll let you have the twenty."

He laughed as he put his gun away and pulled out the flashlight and the envelope he'd stashed in his pockets. After blinding me with a beam of light, he aimed his flash at the envelope, pulled open the flap and peeked inside. He removed a handful of papers, which he carelessly tossed into the backseat. "No fucking money," he grumbled as he sailed the envelope my way. I parted with my twenty, picked up the scattered papers, and jammed them back into the envelope.

Stanley started the car. He turned on the lights and wipers and backed up before pulling out onto Mulholland. I stuck the envelope in my coat pocket and removed my pack of cigarettes. My hand was shaking as I tried to dig out a smoke. I had one cigarette left, but it had been flattened during my fight with Ant.

"Anybody got a smoke?" I asked. "I need something for my nerves."

"Hold on," Jerome said as he reached inside his suit coat. He lit up, inhaled deeply, and passed his cigarette to Stanley, who took a hit and returned it. By the time Jerome reached it back to me, marijuana smoke had filled the car. I cracked my window and took a drag.

"That cigarette suit you, white boy?" Jerome asked.

"I'll let you know in a minute." I coughed as I exhaled the smoke. They both laughed. I'd taken a couple of hits on a reefer at a party once and nodded off. "You guys got me out of a jam and I appreciate it," I managed to say after catching my breath. "That crazy bastard scared the hell out of me." We passed the joint around as we talked. "Last week he tried to run me off the road, and I ended up rolling my car."

"You gotta get new wheels, my man," Jerome said. "You can't be seen driving around town in that wreck. Not if you want any respect."

"And don't park that junker in front of the Charcoal anymore." Stanley looked over his shoulder and snickered. "It's bad for business. Makes it look like lowlifes hang out at the club. Might scare decent people away."

"I happen to have a Dodge sedan," Jerome said to me. "Looks like it just rolled off the assembly line. You could ride in style. My shop is next to the Charcoal. Stop by sometime, and I'll make you a deal."

"Doubt if I could afford it."

"How about a Mercury coupe? Got a few miles on it. We could figure out a payment plan. You know, so much down and so much a month."

"The interest would kill me."

"Okay, I got just the vehicle."

"Hey, peeper," Stanley said, interrupting Jerome's sales pitch. "If we didn't show up, that sucker was gonna whack you. Ain't that right, my man?" They both glanced at me and I nodded solemnly.

"Maybe he just wanted to see if you could fly," Jerome said, chuckling. "We know *he* can't. You're lucky we was in the vicinity, white boy. But what did he have against you, anyway?"

"I know too much."

"What d'you mean?" Jerome said.

"It's hard to explain. He wanted me out of the way. So did his boss. Guess they were worried I might talk to the cops."

"About what?" He turned around and stared at me.

"About Simone being blackmailed over her fling with Nehemiah." I didn't want to go into any details.

"Wait a minute. You telling me that tramp was worried about her reputation?" Jerome snorted. "She was putting out for every other guy she met at the Charcoal."

"Shut up, Jerome," Stanley said.

"What's the matter?" Jerome asked. "You didn't get any?"

Stanley reached over and grabbed Jerome by the front of his coat, and the car swerved briefly before the big man—driving with one hand—steered back into the right lane. "It ain't right to disrespect dead people," he said. "If you can't say nothing decent about the deceased, don't say nothing." Stanley had both hands back on the wheel just in time to avoid careening off the road on the next curve. I didn't hear any more comments about Simone. Stretched out in the backseat, I didn't hear much of anything as I snoozed the rest of the way to my place.

TWENTY-NINE

When I heard a loud bang, I opened my eyes and glimpsed Vincent McGahee and a blonde—most likely Ashley Greene—standing on the front porch of the war hero's Beverly Glen mansion. She looked like the same woman who had stood by Vincent's side at the funeral. Apparently they'd just stepped outside and the screen door had slammed behind them. I hunched down in the front seat of my Ford, which was parked across the street. Ant's comment last night about sniffing around Beverly Glen had brought me here before daylight, but it was well past dawn now.

Oblivious to my presence, the two seemed to be having an argument of some sort. The woman, wearing a purple dress and yellow high heels, turned and quickly descended the steps leading to the driveway, where McGahee's Buick was parked.

"Hey, Ashley, don't act that way," Vincent called after her. He was in his pajamas and slippers. So, it *was* Ashley. No surprise. Then I noticed something a little odd. There wasn't a trace of a limp in Vincent's walk as he followed her down the driveway. Partially paralyzed and in a wheelchair just days ago, he had made a remarkable recovery.

"I don't think you need to go shopping every day," he said.

"Go to hell!" she retorted, pulling keys from her purse and unlocking the driver's door of the Buick.

"You're supposed to be in mourning. It just doesn't look right, darling." Vincent arrived at the car in time to prevent Ashley from opening the door, and the two struggled briefly. He must have soothed her with some sweet talk, which was inaudible to me. At any rate, the two suddenly became cozy. Laughing, she ran her fingers through his hair, and he began shamelessly feeling her up. I squinted, trying to get a better look.

I reached into the glove box and took out my camera just as they began embracing and kissing with the sort of intimacy that seemed totally inappropriate for in-laws. Since the houses on Beverly Glen were separated by high hedges, the couple didn't have to worry about nosy neighbors getting a peek. I brought my camera up and was focusing through my open window when some clown began blowing a car horn. Removing my elbow from the steering wheel, I restored quiet to the neighborhood. But I had failed to get my photograph. The couple quickly separated and anxiously looked my way.

"What the hell do you think you're doing?" Ashley screamed as I held up my camera for her to see.

"Just happened to be in the neighborhood," I said. "Thought I'd stop by to say hello and take a snapshot for the old photo album. I like to keep track of all my former clients. Just a hobby of mine. Hope you're not camera-shy." Vincent came limping down his driveway towards my car. I reached for the ignition key. "Guess your limp just comes and goes—kind of like my backache." The motor wouldn't turn over. He was getting closer, but his apparently sporadic limp was slowing him down some.

"You've got no right to invade our privacy," he said. "I'll take that roll of film." Just as he reached the street, the car finally started.

"I'll send you a print." I stepped on the gas and roared off. I'd let the lovebirds ponder the implications of my surprise visit.

After turning onto Sunset, I paused at the dry cleaners to drop off my brown suit. I was taking it in once a week, about as often as I got roughed up. Then I stopped at Batson's for breakfast and a chat with Betty.

"It's been awhile," she said as she poured my coffee. "A little bird told me you're back in business."

"That little bird's got a big mouth," I said.

"Lucy says you got *two* clients now."

"Which means twice as many headaches."

"Look on the bright side. Now you can afford to treat Lucy in the style she's accustomed to."

"Two dozen clients wouldn't be enough," I said, smiling. "The way that girl spends my money."

"Might not matter anyway. Lucy says she's leery about going out with you. She thinks you're jinxed."

"You talking about what happened on Topanga Canyon?"

"What else?"

"It could happen to anyone."

"But it keeps happening to *you*. She did say she had a swell time once the two of you finally got to Reno." Betty moved on to another table. I looked at Wednesday's *Times*, which I'd picked up at the newsstand around the corner. At the top of the front page was a photo of U.S. bombers in a tight formation as they flew on a mission overseas. Below the fold I found Ben Luper's short article on McGahee's big announcement. It was a PR piece on the old man. There was no mention of my rude question. In a photo, the mayor and the millionaire were holding up the huge cardboard check. I turned the pages and glanced at the headlines before shoving the paper aside.

I wasn't in the mood for reading. I had too much on my mind. I thought about McGahee's right-hand man at the bottom of a deep canyon. Who knew when his body would be found? I'd left Ant's papers in my apartment. I was too tired to give them more than a cursory look last night. There were plenty of scribbled names and numbers. I'd take a closer look later.

I left Betty her usual tip and shut myself inside the phone booth in the back of the coffee house. I fed a nickel into the coin slot. When I got hold of the San Francisco operator, I asked her to put a call through to Ashley Greene's number. Then I changed my mind. "Could you just give me her address?"

"We don't usually give out that information, sir."

"Look, doll, I'm a detective on an urgent case. If you like, I could call my superior to the phone. It would mean getting him out of an important meeting with the mayor and the city council. But if that's what it takes—"

"Twelve forty-five Mallory Street," she said and hung up.

I took Sunset all the way to Pacific Coast Highway and turned right. Last night's rain was long gone, and it was a beautiful day for a lengthy drive up the California coast. The sound of the waves breaking on the shore was music to my ears. When I got to Santa Barbara, I stopped for gasoline and forked over some more of my ration stamps. Then I decided on lunch at a Mexican restaurant, where I ordered a whiskey sour with my enchiladas. It was so cool and restful inside—away from the hot California sun—I decided to relax and order another drink.

I had been putting in too many hours on the job. I needed a little break in order to fully consider this new development in the case: Ashley and Vincent. What did it prove? They were fond of each other. They had lived under the same roof for weeks. They'd shared a common goal: helping Simone. It seemed natural that they would grow close to each other. But how close? Bolstered by another drink, maybe I could put another puzzle piece in place. I stopped kidding myself, called for my check and resumed my trip.

THIRTY

San Francisco was a long drive. I wanted to arrive while it was daylight. I made good time despite having to wait on the side of the road for thirty minutes while a motorcycle cop wrote me a speeding ticket. When he pulled me over, I asked if he wouldn't mind stepping on it, since I had important business to take care of. That's why it took half an hour. At a gas station, I got directions and drove towards my destination. Buildings of different sizes and shapes were crowded together along the city's hilly streets. I made more than a couple of wrong turns before I found the place.

I pulled up in front of Ashley Greene's small two-story house in a neighborhood that had seen better days. I got an old briefcase from the trunk and hurriedly strode up the cracked and crumbling concrete walkway. After climbing the steps to the front porch, I punched the doorbell. On the porch was an ancient rocking chair with a caved-in seat.

While I waited, I took in the view. It probably wouldn't get dark for another hour. Two kids were playing catch with a baseball in front of a nearby house, and an old man way down the street was watering his sparse lawn. A skinny guy, maybe twenty, with a mop of yellow hair, was waxing an old Plymouth coupe parked across the street. Just a typical neighborhood scene. I tried to open the screen door, but it was locked. I took a business card from my wallet and slipped it in between the edge of the door and the frame. After unlatching the hook lock, I pulled the screen door open and turned the handle on the inside door. As I suspected, it was locked.

When I left the porch, the guy across the street was looking my way. I nonchalantly walked along the sidewalk in front of Ashley's house. "Real estate agent," I said, keeping my voice down just in case any nosy neighbors were within earshot. "Just between you and me, buddy, owner's asking way more than it's worth. Especially in this market." He must've bought my gibberish because he just nodded.

"No one answered the door," I quickly added, "but I gotta look the place over anyway. You know, the usual red tape. Nice car you got there."

"Just bought it," he said with a stammer. "Hope I get some time to enjoy it before my number comes up in the draft."

"You got it looking like new."

He was smiling proudly as I turned and followed the walkway around the house to the back door. I guess I was hoping to find some revealing letters from Vincent to his mistress or perhaps some pictures of the lovebirds. I didn't have any idea when their affair had started, but I intended to find out. The screen door was ajar, but the inside door was locked. It looked old and not very sturdy. I turned the handle and thrust my shoulder against the door. It didn't budge more than a hair, and I groaned as a jolt of pain shot down my arm.

"Nobody's home!"

I turned to see an old woman gazing over the rickety, wooden fence that separated the two properties. Wearing a pink nightgown and leaning on a metal walker, she had frizzy white hair and a raspy voice.

"My neighbor's been gone about a month now," she said. "Were you trying to break in, young man?"

"Just trying to see if the door was safely locked."

"All you had to do was turn the handle."

"Also got to make sure the door's sturdy enough to keep out intruders. I'm with Safe Haven Security. Haven't seen any shady-looking characters around, have you?"

"Just you," she replied.

"We got a call to check on the house because the owner's been away for so long. Just a routine safety check. No reason to become alarmed."

"I'm not alarmed, just curious, Mister..." She paused, giving me a distrustful look.

"Raven. Max Raven."

"And you're with Safe Haven Security. Has a nice ring to it."

"Yes, ma'am. Now, I've got to fill out a safety report. Do you know the homeowner personally?"

"Yes. Do you?"

"No. That's why I need the assistance of someone as keenly observant as yourself."

"Boy, are you full of B.S.," she said with a snort.

"Well, if you don't want to lend a hand, that's okay." I started to walk away.

"Exactly what do you want to know?" she asked, curiosity perhaps getting the best of her.

"To provide first-rate security we need to know some facts about homeowners and their habits."

"Why don't you just ask the homeowner?"

"We like to check with the neighbors to verify our information. Now, how long have you known the homeowner?" I put down my briefcase, opened it, and took out a clipboard. I got a pencil from my pocket and started scribbling as she answered my questions.

"I've known Ashley since she was a child. That's when the Pearsons moved here. I watched her and her older sister grow up. Too bad what happened to Simone—dying the way she did in a car wreck. I always liked her best. She was always so gloomy, but she was never rude like her sister."

"This was Ashley and Simone's childhood home?"

She nodded.

"Where are the parents?" I asked.

"Killed in a car wreck. Guess it runs in the family. But that was after the girls were grown and living on their own. Ashley moved back into the house with her husband, but they got divorced soon afterwards. Think she mostly lives off her alimony payments. Works as a secretary sometimes. Simone was an actress, you know, and lived in Hollywood. I don't get out much anymore, so I haven't seen any of her movies in a long time."

"When's the last time you saw Simone in person?"

"Let's see. I saw her just after they bombed Pearl Harbor. She married that oil tycoon's boy and brought him to San Francisco for their honeymoon. They stayed here for a couple of weeks. Guess she wanted to show him around her hometown." She smiled, apparently enjoying the opportunity to talk to someone. "When they got back to Hollywood, I heard he joined the Army and went overseas to fight the Nazis. Now he's a war hero."

"Did Simone ever visit her sister during her husband's time overseas?"

"Yes, she dropped in a couple times, but that was a while ago."

"Anything else you'd like to tell me, ma'am?"

"Call me Lizzie. I'm just getting to the good part, Mr. Raven. Simone's husband must've got a furlough one time, because I recall him visiting Ashley by himself, you know, without his wife. About a year ago. Don't you think that's odd, Mr. Raven?"

"Yes, Lizzie, I think that's odd." The long trip had made me drowsy, but I was wide awake now.

"He was just one of many gentlemen callers over the years. I've lost track of how many. Anyway, I didn't approve of all her carrying on, and I told her so. We're not on speaking terms anymore. Haven't been for some time now." She stopped to catch her breath.

"You've been a great help, Lizzie."

"Wait a minute, Mr. Raven. I saved the best for last. I made a long-distance call to Simone when her husband was visiting Ashley. I thought she ought to know what's what with them two."

"What'd she say when you told her?"

"She pretended everything was okay. She's a good actress, but she didn't fool me none. I could tell she was broken up about it."

"Nothing gets by you, does it, Lizzie?"

"I don't pay much attention to things the way I used to. Not since my stroke. Don't read the newspaper anymore. Get most all my news off the radio. Read my Bible and pray every day our troops will come home safely after defeating Hitler and them."

The old lady's back door swung open, and she turned her head to take a look. I eased around to the side of Ashley's house, but I forgot my briefcase. I noticed the guy with the Plymouth was backing his shiny car into the street. Maybe he wanted to show it off to his friends. We waved to each other as he drove off. Then I turned and peeked around the corner of the house.

"Miss Hicks, what on earth are you doing?" asked a middle-aged woman in a nurse's uniform. I watched as she walked over to the old lady. Then I ducked out of sight and listened.

"Why, I'm just helping out this young gentleman," Lizzie replied. "Answering some questions for him."

"You need to come back inside right now!" the nurse ordered. "I don't see anyone."

"Well, he was here just a minute ago." Lizzie sounded baffled. "He was right next door."

"Just as I thought, Miss Hicks," the nurse said condescendingly. "You're conjuring up apparitions to talk to again. You gotta stop wandering off every time I turn my back."

"Take a look over there, why don't you?" Lizzie said. "Right by our neighbor's back door. Did I conjure *that* up?"

"What is it? Looks like a briefcase."

"The man left it when he ran away."

"Why would he run away?"

"When he heard you coming, he must've gotten scared. He's probably a criminal. And I fell for his line about being with some security company. We gotta call the police."

"Calm down, Miss Hicks," the nurse said firmly. "Let's get you back into the house."

"We better hurry or he'll get away."

"Careful, Miss Hicks. Now, watch your step."

As they walked away, I jumped out and retrieved my briefcase. I stuck my clipboard back inside. Rushing back to my car, I couldn't help laughing at Lizzie's reaction to my disappearing act. I was just glad I didn't have to deal with her cranky nurse. A headache hadn't hit me yet today. I wanted to keep it that way.

I drove off thinking about my next move. Simone got Lizzie's fateful phone call about the time she started showing up at the clubs on Central. Coincidence or a reaction to her husband's infidelity? Something to ponder as I drove back to L.A. But first I decided to hit a seafood restaurant and indulge my sudden appetite for lobster. Afterwards I'd take in the sights.

THIRTY-ONE

My sightseeing tour of San Francisco didn't even get as far as the Golden Gate Bridge. I spent the night barhopping and then checked into a waterfront hotel. My early morning start got me back in L.A. by Thursday afternoon. I picked up my suit from the cleaners and grabbed a *Times* from the newsstand. During a late lunch at the coffee house, I browsed the front page.

Yesterday, the strangler had struck again. But he came up empty-handed this time. His intended victim, Tina Ferrante, escaped when an undercover cop intervened. The cop broke both legs and an arm when the strangler flung him off Tina's balcony. The actress managed to take refuge inside her apartment, but the strangler was still on the loose. Tina was unharmed. Presumably, the cop was resting uncomfortably in a local hospital. Just another day in the big city. The newspaper ran photos of both of them along with a sketch of the alleged strangler. He almost looked familiar. The cop was definitely the guy I roughed up a few days ago. Now the strangler had manhandled him. Maybe he should find another line of work. McGahee's fifty-grand offer was still open for alert citizens, the paper said. I didn't find any item about Ant, his automobile or my missing .45 in the paper, and breathed a premature sigh of relief.

I was ready to resume my investigation. Finishing my coffee, I folded the newspaper and tucked it under my arm. I paid my check, and on my way out I waved to Betty, who was just coming off her break. I'd been seeing more of Betty than of her sister-in-law. Actually, I hadn't seen Lucy since the weekend. We had talked on the phone a couple of times. Since our work schedules were different, it was difficult to get together. Besides, my cash reserves had dwindled after we'd splurged in Reno.

As I walked to my car, Detective Drayton and a uniformed cop suddenly appeared, one on each side of me. "You're under arrest, Craven," said Drayton, a fat cigar wobbling in his mouth as he talked. He took custody of my newspaper. "Put your hands behind your back. Cuff him, Sergeant Freedy."

"What for?" I asked as I reluctantly complied.

"You'll find out when we get to the station." After being handcuffed, I was led to an unmarked police car. As the sergeant opened the back door, Drayton shoved me inside. He got in the front passenger side, and then the sergeant drove us over to Central Division.

On the way, I asked, "What's the charge? Carrying a newspaper without a permit? Failure to fold it properly?"

"Enough with the lame wisecracks," Drayton barked. That ended our conversation. Once at the police station, I was taken to an interrogation room, where he unlocked my handcuffs. We sat across from each other at a metal table.

"We found a bullet-riddled Lincoln crashed at the bottom of Mulholland Drive this morning," he said, puffing on his sick-making cigar and blowing smoke in my face. "Underneath the car, we found the driver's crushed body. It was also riddled with bullets. Does the name Anthony Prior mean anything to you? He's a convicted felon wanted on a parole violation."

I shrugged.

"We found two guns nearby." Drayton aimed a finger at me. "One was a snub-nosed .38 with the serial number filed off, and the other one was a Colt .45. We ran a check on the Colt's serial number. Any idea who it's registered to?"

"I wouldn't be surprised if it's mine. I own a Colt .45, and a hoodlum named Ant took it away from me."

"Ant?"

"That's what they called your dead guy. He worked for Victor McGahee. His bodyguard. I recently had a meeting with Mr. McGahee in connection with the case I'm working on. Before we sat down to chat, Ant relieved me of my weapon. That's how he got my gun. Why don't you call the old man? I'm sure he'll be happy to vouch for me," I said sarcastically. "That's about all I know." That wasn't exactly the truth. Maybe McGahee didn't know that Ant had returned my gun. Of course, the gangster had taken it away again later that night. I wasn't really counting on McGahee to bail me out. Learning about my predicament would probably make his day.

"You're saying this guy Prior worked for the oil tycoon?" Drayton asked.

"That's right. McGahee's probably wondering what in the world happened to his missing bodyguard."

"When did you meet with McGahee?"

"Tuesday, about noon, at the Beverly Hills Hotel. The waiter working the lounge will remember me."

"For a grimy gumshoe, you get around, don't you?"

"What can I tell you?" I said, smiling.

"Here's what I can tell *you*," Drayton said. "In a two-week period, we found two people along with their automobiles at the bottom of two canyons. And you had encounters with both victims shortly before they were killed. First we find Simone Pearson's body, and then the body of some guy you say worked for her father-in-law."

"The world's riddled with coincidences."

"You're not employed by the old man's son anymore. So, who's your new client?" he demanded.

I ignored his question and asked one of my own. "You working the Pearson case again?"

"It's been more or less in limbo since we found out the strangler didn't do it. The wheels downtown are sure it was an accident or a suicide and just want us to move on. We don't have any leads that indicate otherwise. But I got a hunch it just might of been murder." He leaned over the table and snickered. "Tell you what, Sid. Give me whatever clues you got. I'll check 'em out and let you know if you're on the right track. You want to help me catch the killer, don't you? It'll be just like old times."

"You couldn't nab the killer if he surrendered to you."

Drayton got up, angrily yanked opened the door and hollered, "Sergeant Freedy!" When the sergeant arrived, Drayton said, "Put this SOB in a holding cell until I can check on his story about his missing gun." I was roughly led away by Freedy, who took me downstairs and placed me in a large jail cell with two other prisoners. They looked about twenty. Both wore blue suits and fedoras. They'd been huddled in a corner, where they were playing a dice game. But they stopped to check out my arrival.

"Don't I get a phone call?" I asked as Freedy slammed the cell door shut.

"Phone's out of order, Dime Detective," he said, walking away.

"*You're* out of order," one of my cellmates called after him. "What'd they get you for?" he asked me.

"Failure to do their jobs for 'em." I didn't feel like having a conversation about my arrest.

"Huh?"

"They expect me to solve crimes for free."

"I don't get it."

"I'm a private detective. I don't work for the police."

"Hey, I recognize your face. Your photo was on the front page of that tabloid. What did that cop call you just now?" He paused while he did some thinking. "I just figured it out. You're the Dime Detective."

"I guess everybody and his uncle must read that crappy paper."

"The cops asked for *your* help? They must really be hurting, huh?"

"You're a smart guy."

"Not smart enough to stay out of jail."

"What are you in for?" I asked, changing the subject.

"They're charging me and my buddy here with passing counterfeit ten-dollar bills."

"How'd they catch you?"

"We purchased a used Chevy last week. The damn muffler fell off. When we took the clunker back, they nabbed us. The guy who sold us the car called the cops. They're claiming we bought it with phony ten-dollar bills."

"Did you?" I asked.

"Just a case of mistaken identity. We paid for that overpriced rattletrap with a stack of singles. Didn't we, Andy?"

"Absolutely, Tommy," his partner said.

"Now they're checking to see if we're draft dodgers. Once they start looking around, you never know what they'll try to pin on you. We told 'em we both had medical deferments. They don't believe us." Tommy rattled a pair of dice in his fist. "Wanna join us in a game of chance? You might win some big money."

"What are you playing with? Tens?"

"Very funny. The cops took away all our money. We're using match sticks. We'll settle up with real cash when we get out."

"I'd like to join you, but my girl wouldn't like it."

"Why's that?"

"She wouldn't want me gambling away money I could be spending on *her*."

"Come on, Andy, you ready to roll 'em?"

"Positively," his companion responded. They resumed their game. I walked over and stretched out on a bench against a wall on the other side of the jail cell. As they grumbled and exchanged obscenities, I slid my hat down over my face and shut my eyes. In a few minutes I dozed off. I dreamed I was on a boat tossed by high waves in a storm. A woman had fallen overboard, or perhaps she'd jumped or been pushed. Since no one else was willing to rescue her, I plunged into the turbulent waters and wrapped my arms tightly around her. But she wrenched away, pushed me under the water, and swam to safety as the waves carried me off.

I was awakened when Freedy unlocked the cell door and banged it open. He took me up to Drayton's office. The detective, who was on the phone when I entered the room, motioned me to a chair. Hanging up, he said, "You're free to go, Craven, on one condition: drop your investigation into Simone Pearson's death. We just got the word. The case is officially closed. Besides, the coroner's already ruled out homicide."

"Perhaps, he's mistaken," I said with a cagey smile. "Maybe the cops don't have all the facts."

"I'll play along. What do you know that the police don't?"

Suddenly I felt an urge to explain why the cops were making a big mistake in not pursuing their investigation. "I heard rumors there might be some hanky-panky going on between the husband and sister-in-law at the Beverly Glen house. She's younger than the Pearson frail was. Could be Vincent wanted his wife out of the way. And maybe his wheelchair's just a prop to divert suspicion away from him."

"You're not trying to pin it on your former client, are you? You know, I wouldn't mind nailing that rich boy myself if I thought I could."

"A spouse is the most likely suspect."

"Forget it, Sid," Drayton said with regret. "The war hero has a solid alibi. The sister, too. They were at home on the Friday Simone vanished. Her sister went to the beauty parlor early in the afternoon. We verified her appointment. She was gone about an hour. They both stayed at home the rest of the day. We checked with the neighbors. We talked to the butler. He was with them until eight. That's when he left for the night. Are you following my train of thought?"

"I'm waiting for it to arrive at the depot." I purposely yawned.

"Now," he said, "the Pearson broad apparently got drunk and wrecked her car not too long after she scuffled with you at Muriel's. She was killed in the crash no later than five o'clock on that Friday afternoon. The coroner thinks so anyway. Our war hero and Simone's sister didn't have time to commit the crime, even if he *wasn't* an invalid. For the record, it's about an hour's drive from the Beverly Glen residence to the crash site up in the mountains. I drove it myself, and I didn't hit much traffic. Keep in mind that the round trip would take twice as long—longer with traffic. Not that it matters. The two of them were home when Simone's car went into that canyon. No way they could of pulled it off. Now, that's first-rate police work. I believe I just nailed down all the pertinent facts." He gave me a wide smile.

"I was hoping you'd tell me something I don't already know," I said. But I might have learned a thing or two from his rambling narrative. I'd sort it out later. "What if I stumbled onto some new evidence?"

"Sidney, you're not listening. Take your pick: accident or suicide."

"Come on, Nick, I thought you were looking for the truth. Now you're trying to cover it up."

"Lay off the case, Craven," Drayton said, ignoring my accusation. "You're just taking your client for a ride."

"What's it to you? Is this a message from your captain?"

He shook his head. "Higher up. I'm telling you for your own good. Go out and get stinking drunk. Do whatever you want. Just drop the case."

"And if I don't?"

"There's the matter of your .45 found next to Prior's body. Lucky for you, we couldn't get any readable fingerprints from the gun. But we're gonna run ballistics tests to determine if any of the bullets we found in his corpse or in his car came from your weapon."

"Your tests can't prove who *fired* the weapon. Anyway, whoever killed that snake did you a favor."

"We also found all sorts of spent cartridges next to Mulholland, where we believe the shooters were waiting to ambush Prior as he drove by. Some of the shells were from a .45."

"You got me." I held out my hands for him to cuff me. "After my gang bumped off Prior, I tossed my gun into the canyon so the cops could find it. I forgot what my motive was."

Drayton ignored my sarcasm. "Look, Sid, if nothing else, we got you as an accomplice in the murder of Anthony Prior."

"I already told you Prior took my gun. Did McGahee back me up when you called him?"

"The captain talked to him."

"What did he say?"

"The call was to inform McGahee about his bodyguard. They didn't have time for small talk. The old guy's time is valuable. What did you expect?"

"Bet McGahee took the time to call his good buddy the mayor. Here's what I think. The SOB almost had a stroke when he heard about his right-hand man. Now there's another police investigation that might entangle him. He just wants it all to go away. And when he talks, the mayor listens. Let me get this straight," I said disgustedly. "You'll just forget about finding my weapon at the Mulholland crime scene if I stop looking into Simone Pearson's death?"

"You said it, Sid, not me. Now what's it gonna be?"

"You win." I slowly got to my feet.

As I walked out the door and down the hall, Drayton followed me. "You were in way over your head, Craven. Now you'll probably live longer." He laughed. Maybe he was right, but I'd have to live with myself.

THIRTY-TWO

Night was falling as I stood outside the police station. I hailed a taxi, which had just dropped off a stern-looking, elderly gentleman with an ornately carved walking stick. Perhaps he was here to bail out a wayward son or daughter, or maybe he was a criminal turning himself in before the authorities could nab him. Maybe he was making a payoff to some crooked cop. Who knew what nasty little secrets were hidden behind someone's frown or smile? Who knew when someone was telling the truth, the whole truth, and nothing but the truth? Or when someone was lying to get out of a jam or to protect someone or to frame someone? Or when someone was just suffering a memory lapse? Who the hell knew? Not me. I was just a weary soul on my way home after a long day.

The cabbie dropped me in front of Batson's, where I picked up my car. It was after nine when I finally drove into the parking lot of my apartment building. After a shower, I heated up a can of beef stew. I had reached my quota of canned foods for June. But I'd get more ration stamps next week.

Dressed in my favorite suit, but feeling naked without my Colt, I drove over to the Twilight Lounge to kill the rest of the evening. Sipping my second drink and puffing on a Chesterfield, I soon forgot Drayton's warning about the Pearson case. I was engaged in a somewhat one-sided conversation with the shapely brunette on the bar stool next to mine when I caught a glimpse of a familiar face. Since the brunette had basically lost interest in me from the moment I said hello, I found it easy to excuse myself and slip away. I snuffed out my cigarette and took my drink and my hat.

Without so much as an invitation, I joined fat Bert Brenley, who was conversing with two sexy young babes at a corner table.

"What the hell do *you* want?" he said rudely.

"Just a few questions I'd like to ask you, Mr. Brenley. You do remember me, don't you?"

"Should I?"

"You snapped my photo at Empire Studios and gave me a big write-up in your paper. It wasn't exactly flattering, but then you failed to get *my* side of the story."

"You're that lame detective who couldn't find his own shadow on a sunny day." Both girls giggled. "I don't have time for losers," he added. "Come on, drift. Take a hike."

"Your girlfriends might be interested in learning about a somewhat unorthodox activity of yours involving a recently deceased actress."

"Could you please excuse us, girls?" Brenley said. "Give me about five minutes to straighten this guy out."

"Well, I guess we could go powder our noses," one of the girls suggested.

"That's a swell idea." Brenley watched them stroll towards the restroom. Then he turned to me. "Okay, Craven, what the fuck are you trying to pull? That was you who called me on the phone earlier in the week—making those ludicrous allegations—wasn't it?"

The other day my temper had flared. Today I was determined to stay calm. "Anthony Prior's dead," I said indifferently.

"Who?" His eyebrows jumped. He lit a cigarette, took a drag, and then placed it in the ashtray next to the one he already had going. Then he quickly picked up the half-smoked cigarette and snubbed it out.

I lit one of my Chesterfields. "Looks like you're suddenly a little jumpy. Simone and Prior were part of your blackmail scheme. Now, both are dead. Perhaps you're next."

"Are you threatening me?"

"I'm just warning you. If you don't tell me what *you* know, I'm going to the police with what *I* know."

"They wouldn't believe you of all people."

"Maybe not, but they'll probably call you in for questioning and make trouble for you."

"I doubt it. They'd figure you were just trying to get back at me for my reporting, which exposed you as a bungling detective. Hell, you were fired from the D.A.'s office for drinking on the job, weren't you? With your reputation—"

"Maybe the cops would believe Faye Fluellen." That stopped him as quickly as a bullet in the head. "You found out I was looking for Faye that day you ran into me at Empire. But you failed to mention that detail in your story because you knew the cops would question her. Faye was the one who gave you the dope on Simone. She was onto your blackmail scheme. If they got her to talk, you might find yourself in a tight spot."

He looked around and waved off the two girls, who were returning from the john. They retreated, taking seats at the bar, where they were immediately joined by two leering sailors.

"If I tell you what I know," he said, "you might still go to the police."

"Guess you'll have to trust *me* just like Simone had to trust *you*. Come on, Brenley. Talk to me about blackmail. Tell me what you know about Prior. How did he fit into your scheme?" I was beginning to sound like Drayton. This case was wearing me down.

"Ant tailed Simone to our meeting place," he said.

"You mean the place where Simone handed over your hush money?" My voice was full of scorn.

"Not so loud." He quickly glanced around. "After Simone, uh, slipped me the cash and took off—that's when Ant braced me. He introduced himself and then demanded half the money."

"I *figured* he tracked you down. Why didn't you just tell him to hit the road?"

"You don't tell that scary motherfucker what to do. He threatened to kill me. He wanted to find out what I knew about Simone and her boyfriend. Ant's the hatchet man for Victor McGahee, Simone's father-in-law. The oil magnate was coughing up the hush money, and Ant was cutting himself in. He said the old man wanted me rubbed out. But Ant was stalling while he picked up some easy money. He's got me looking over my shoulder whenever I hear footsteps." Brenley wiped his sweaty brow with a handkerchief. "How do you know he's dead?"

"Your buddy Detective Drayton told me. Ant was killed in a shootout.

I'm not sure what facts the police have released to the press yet."

"I wouldn't know, since I've been busy working on the crime story of the decade." He puffed on his cigarette. "I've spent two hectic days knocking on doors and tracking down witnesses for the strangler series we've been running. They almost caught him this time. Didn't you see my front-page story in today's *Mirror*? I interviewed Tina Ferrante and the hero cop with the broken limbs. We ran a blowup of the police sketch of the strangler. Tomorrow's paper will have more exclusive details."

"I don't read your trashy tabloid anymore," I told Brenley, who showed me the ring on his fat middle finger—or maybe he was just giving me the finger. "Let's get back to the subject of extortion. Why'd you think you could get away with it?"

"For starters, I knew I couldn't get the money from Simone. She had just been fired by her studio. Anyway, she was a contract player, not really a big star. She would have to tap the old man for the amount of cash I wanted. I figured if the rumors about him cheating his investors were true, he'd come across with the funds. He wouldn't take the chance that a scandal involving his daughter-in-law might lead to meddling reporters exposing his questionable business practices. You know how one thing leads to another. And I could've pulled it off without a hitch. But Prior had to horn in," he said ruefully. I had to give Brenley credit. He certainly had the old man figured out.

"Didn't Simone ever try to get you to hand over the negative of your blackmail photo?" I said.

"Uh-huh. Whenever I talked to her on the phone. But I reminded her this wasn't the movies. Real blackmailers always keep the negative and extra prints. Simone knew she was in a bind. She'd have to keep asking the old man to shell out more hush money."

"How'd Simone drop off the payments?"

"She'd just hand me a folded-up newspaper with the cash inside. Wouldn't say a word to me."

"How much money we talking about?"

"I'll tell you this much. The gangster always showed up and took his cut. But Simone shorted me more than once. With all the shit she was going through, I figured she was entitled to skim some pocket money for herself.

I mean, she was starting to look really frazzled. So I never called her on it."

Bighearted Bert Brenley. I almost wanted to shake his sweaty hand. I cringed at the thought. He anxiously looked around the place, brought out his sopping handkerchief, and again mopped his forehead. Brenley acted as if he thought his former partner in crime might be alive and within striking distance.

"How many payments did Simone make?" I asked.

"Not many. Maybe four or five. Prior was running the show. He'd get in touch when he wanted more cash. I'd phone Simone, and she'd let me know when she got the money. We'd meet right here at the Twilight Lounge. But then Ant decided to back off."

"Why?"

"He found out her husband was returning from the war. Ant thought it would be best to lay low. He figured it was too risky. The husband might find out, and the whole thing could blow up in our faces."

"*Did* he find out? After all, his own father was paying the hush money."

"How would I know? That's one hell of a peculiar family."

"Did you tell Simone you were letting her off the hook?"

"I figured she got the message when I stopped calling her." He looked down at the ashtray, where both our cigarettes were smoldering. "I felt awful when I learned she died in a car crash."

"Fuck off, Brenley," I said, taking one last drag from my Chesterfield and standing up. I considered spitting on the bloated bastard, but instead I flicked my cigarette at him. It landed inside his suit coat. He rocked back in his chair as he frantically attempted to brush the lit butt from his clothes. When the chair started tipping over backwards, he began flailing his arms in an effort to reverse his momentum and stay upright. For such a hefty man it was bound to be a losing struggle. I took my hat and walked towards the exit. I heard a woman shriek and the sound of wood splintering when Brenley—along with his chair—crashed to the floor. All his flab probably cushioned his fall.

THIRTY-THREE

On Friday morning, the *Times* carried a brief piece on the death of Anthony Prior. I read the story over a plate of waffles and some coffee at Batson's. Prior had done time in Texas on a racketeering conviction. Released early from prison, he'd violated his parole by leaving the state. Efforts by authorities to track him down had failed until yesterday when police discovered his bullet-riddled body pinned under his shot-up vehicle in the canyon below Mulholland Drive.

Ant's violent gangland slaying was perhaps retaliation by some of his old rivals or former cronies from Houston, according to a police spokesman. Apparently, Prior had been ambushed by gunmen while he was driving along Mulholland and then lost control of his vehicle, which careened off the road and over the canyon side. Numerous shell casings—from the weapons used in the attack—were found on the side of the road. How the victim's body wound up *under* his vehicle was a mystery detectives were still puzzling over.

His employer Victor McGahee told police that Prior had held a low-level security position with McGahee Enterprises. McGahee denied any knowledge of Prior's criminal record and said he was instituting a new company policy—effective immediately—which called for extensive background checks prior to any future hiring. No other details were disclosed about the killing. The police were treating it like a mob shooting.

Betty refilled my coffee cup. "How's your big case coming along, Sid?"

"I'm about ready to wrap it up," I said, exhaling a plume of smoke.

"You mean you're not gonna milk it for a few extra bucks?" She laughed.

"No way. Today's the day."

"Sure, Sid," she said jokingly. "If you say so."

"Why don't we go out to a club tonight and celebrate? Lucy's got to work. You could be her double, you know, like in the movies. Tell your hubby to give you the night off. Just a little dancing, a little drinking. I'll show you a good time. All you got to do is loosen up a touch." I showed her a five and slid it under my plate.

"You're wasting your breath *and* your money," she said. We both laughed.

In the lobby of my office building, I passed right by the mailboxes on my way to the elevator. I wasn't in the mood for any bills or annoying advertisements today. I opened my office window and turned on the floor fan in an attempt to rid the place of the stale air that had accumulated in my absence. Tossing my hat and newspaper on the desk, I sat down in my chair. I opened my desk drawer and took out my flimsy file on the Pearson case. It contained some scribbled notes, newspaper clippings on the police investigation, and the glossy publicity photo. Maybe I'd missed something. I took another look at the coroner's findings from last week's *Times*. Then I closed the file folder and put it away.

I took out Ant's dog-eared manila envelope from my coat pocket and dumped the contents onto my desk. There were about a dozen pages, which looked like they'd been torn from some kind of accounting book. I saw a bunch of names along with dollar amounts. I wondered if the documents might implicate McGahee in any wrongdoing. Maybe they were Ant's idea of an insurance policy. Luckily, Stanley had looked in the hoodlum's glove box. If the cops ever got their hands on these papers, they'd probably never see the light of day.

After shrugging out of my suit coat, I called the *Times*. I gave the secretary my name and asked for Ben Luper. I'd never met the guy, but maybe we could do some business. When he picked up, I explained that I was working on the Pearson case.

"Yeah, the Dime Detective," he said, laughing. "I tried to get a comment from you last week for my story, but I guess you were unavailable."

"I'm available now. And I've got some financial documents you might want to take a look at. I believe they're records of Victor McGahee's wheeling and dealing."

"How'd you get *your* hands on 'em?"

"Let's just say one of his employees didn't object to my getting hold of the documents. His name was Anthony Prior. I think he was worried that something might happen to him. By any chance, did you read your own paper today?"

"That's the guy killed on Mulholland."

"Yeah, I met him on the Pearson case. Maybe he had good reason to be concerned. Here's the deal. I'll give you the documents. Just don't say you got 'em from me."

"Exactly what do you have?"

"Bookkeeping isn't my strong point," I admitted. "Maybe you can figure it out. You're the ace reporter."

"We've been trying to get something on that slippery SOB for years."

"Really? I couldn't tell by reading that PR piece you wrote about his city hall appearance."

"*Now* I recognize your voice," he said. "You're the wise guy who asked McGahee that last question from the back of the crowd, aren't you?"

"Nobody else was asking tough questions. He was just getting free publicity."

"That publicity may just cost him fifty grand," Luper noted. "My reason for covering the press conference was to tell our readers about McGahee's reward offer—not to slander the man. Now, if you got some *proof* of his wrongdoing, that's another matter."

"When are you free?"

"I usually take lunch at twelve-thirty," he said. I gave him my address, and he told me he'd drop by.

I dialed Simone's former agent Harrison Hammerman. His secretary said he was busy. I informed her I was a detective on an important case that involved one of his clients.

"Which client?" she asked.

"Simone Pearson."

There was a pause before she responded. "Miss Pearson's no longer a client."

"Look, I'm at the airport. I'm in a phone booth overlooking the runway. My flight's about to leave." I rolled up a section of the newspaper, reached over, and stuck it in the fan.

"What's that noise?" she asked.

"An airplane just taxied by. *My* plane's next." I tossed the shredded newspaper back on the desk.

"*That* was an airplane?"

"I've only got a few minutes."

"Hold on," she said. I propped my feet on the desk and waited patiently.

"Hammerman here. What's so goddamn important you got to interrupt me? I'm with a client."

"Mr. Hammerman. Sidney Craven. I'm investigating Simone Pearson's death. I'd like to ask you a couple of questions."

"Why should I take time out of my busy schedule to talk with *you*?"

"Maybe you'd like to help me find out what really happened to your former client. Maybe you want to see justice done. Maybe you have a conscience. Or don't you give a damn?"

"All right," he said. "Ask away, but make it snappy."

"You were Simone's agent. What can you tell me about trying to get her showbiz career back on track?"

"A couple of weeks ago, Victor McGahee called. In case you don't already know, that's her father-in-law. He asked if I'd represent her. McGahee's my investment banker, and he's making me a shitload of money. But let's face it. Simone had been in some flops recently. That's probably why Empire didn't have any qualms about firing her in the first place. She just walks out on the movie she's shooting. Says she has pneumonia. Then shows up at the studio and lambastes the director for replacing her. This director has a giant ego and lots of clout. Not to mention he's a vindictive asshole. He doesn't appreciate being shown up in front of the whole cast and crew. He makes some phone calls. Soon the Hollywood grapevine's buzzing with the news about Simone Pearson's erratic behavior. You know, she's unreliable and prone to tantrums on the set."

"That's bullshit, right?" I said.

"She was probably just guilty of speaking her mind to the wrong guy. The director claimed she was drunk, and maybe she was. Hollywood thrives on rumors. The tabloids did a real number on her. Facts don't count with them. They wanna sell papers. None of the studios would touch her for the time being. Simone must have felt resentful. Who wouldn't? Heard she started going to auditions when she was hammered."

"With all the gossip out there, how do you know *what* to believe about Simone?"

"It's my job to keep tabs on the Hollywood scene," Hammerman said. "And I get all my info straight from the horse's mouth. I'm talking to studio bosses every day. Of course, you can't believe *everything* you hear. Anyway, McGahee told me Simone had been sober for about a month. Said she had some kind of religious experience that turned her life around. Hey, anything can happen in Hollywood. We love a comeback story. I had a feeling the time was right for Simone. So I agreed to sign her up for the old man's sake. After all, she *was* a wonderful actress. She had a wacky comedy style along with a touch of glamour. You don't find that every day. Those morons over at Empire didn't know how to properly manage someone with Simone's talent. I could have guided her comeback and turned her into a genuine movie star." He paused, as if savoring the thought.

"How'd you swing an audition for her?"

"Simone showed up at my office and signed on the dotted line. We didn't talk about her past troubles. But I warned her it wasn't gonna be easy finding a director who'd work with her because of all the buzz." He hesitated briefly. "Then the very same day, I got a call from a director at Empire of all places. He needed an emergency replacement for an actress. Who knows why? She probably refused to sleep with him and quit when he kept hounding her. Anyway, the guy just happened to owe me a favor. Once I got the studio's approval, I sent Simone over and she landed the part. She called and thanked me profusely. She went to rehearsals but then didn't show up the next day. I got an earful from the director. Her conduct reflects on me personally. I got my reputation to think about."

"What about *her* reputation?" I asked. "Maybe she *didn't* drunkenly or purposely kill herself. When was the last time you spoke with her?" There was a moment of silence on the line.

"Simone called me up one night," Hammerman finally said. "She had just returned home from rehearsals."

"That was the night before she disappeared."

"Uh, yeah. I guess so. She sounded distraught." He paused again. "She'd just found her husband and her sister, uh, in bed. Apparently they were going at it like their license to commit adultery was about to expire. And he's supposed to be paralyzed. Simone told me she'd been aware of their affair, but now she had the proof she'd been looking for. She asked for my advice. Hell, I'm the last person to ask about marriage problems. I'm going through a messy divorce even as we speak. I told her to call me in the morning when she calmed down, and I'd give her the name of my wife's lawyer. I figured since he's running circles around *my* attorney and getting everything I got, he might as well clean out Simone's husband. She was sobbing and carrying on. It was hard to understand her. Then she just hung up. She may have been drunk. That's the last time I talked to her. If you ask me, she was overwrought and suicidal. Good luck trying to prove otherwise. Look, I got a call on the other line." He hung up.

Five minutes later, the phone rang. It was Wesley Renfro. He wanted to know what I had turned up on the Pearson case.

"It wasn't accidental," I said with confidence.

"What evidence you got?"

"She was hospitalized for depression and drug addiction. She underwent electroshock therapy."

"That's experimental treatment, isn't it?" he asked, excitement creeping into his voice. "I mean it hasn't been proven completely effective."

"What's your point?"

"My *point*, Sid, is that it obviously didn't work in Simone Pearson's case. Maybe it had just the opposite result. I mean, instead of curing her, it drove her to suicide." He was definitely excited. "Where'd you get your information from?"

I told him I'd taken a glimpse at Simone's medical file at the Wamsley Center in Glendale. Then I mentioned her agent's late-night phone conversation with her. "Believe it or not, I got the tip about her electroshock therapy from the old man's bodyguard. His name's Anthony Prior. You may have read about him in the paper this morning."

"The gangster who was gunned down?"

"At least he won't be able to deny what he told me," I said jokingly.

"He's not a reliable source, anyway," Renfro said. "Okay, so you've given me Dr. Wamsley's diagnosis of Miss Pearson's condition. Sounds like she was a suicide waiting to happen. That's enough for Uptowner to refuse payment of the thirty grand. If it winds up in court, we'll get Wamsley to testify about his diagnosis *and* his treatment of her. If necessary, we'll call her agent to the stand to describe her mental state the night before she killed herself. Good job, Sid. We've got a solid case."

"There may be a better case for murder."

"Don't tell me you think the husband did it," he said with a snicker.

"He just may be involved. I've been looking into it. Give me one more day. Wouldn't you rather have an airtight homicide than an iffy suicide?"

"Remember, Sid, I hired you to look into a suicide, not to go chasing after clues to implicate a crippled war hero in the dubious murder of his wife. Sounds like you're doing research for one of your detective stories. Just don't charge me for whatever time you put in on your homicide investigation."

"A grand jury may disagree with your take on the case."

"What do I care? Uptowner wins anyway. Now, what do I owe you, Sidney?"

"Let's see. You called me last Thursday, but I didn't put myself on the clock until Friday. I take weekends off."

"Come on," he said impatiently, "just give me an estimate."

"I'd say I spent three days working on the suicide angle for you. Then on Wednesday, I began looking into the possibility it was a homicide."

"Okay, then bill me for three days."

"That comes to, uh, ninety dollars on the nose."

"You said twenty-five a day."

"Plus expenses," I reminded him. "The extra fifteen includes the cost of phone calls and gasoline for the trip to Glendale. Also a dry-cleaning bill and a new hat."

"You can't charge for those last two items."

"Why not?" I protested. "Without the proper attire, I can't do my job. I had to look the part of a respectable researcher in order to finagle my way into the hospital to get a look at Simone Pearson's medical records. Not to mention I had to bribe the receptionist."

"I didn't hear that, Sid. You know I'm only authorized to reimburse you for your lawful expenses. Counting the gas and the phone bill, let's call it eighty. Give me a ring when you get a confession from the husband, and we'll talk. By the way, what evidence you got against him?"

"That'll cost you, Wes."

He chuckled and hung up. Too bad I couldn't sell Renfro on the murder angle. He acted as if the extra fee would have come out of his own pocket. Of course, Uptowner would've paid the bill. Maybe he got a bonus for keeping expenses down. Nehemiah had come up with a hell of a lot more money, but *he* wanted me to search for a killer.

THIRTY-FOUR

I phoned the Red-Hot Charcoal, but the bandleader wasn't in. A call to Vincent McGahee's number got me a busy signal. Lucy didn't answer her phone. Then I remembered Friday was her day to go shopping. It was about noon. Taking my hat and coat, I went out for a stroll and grabbed a quick lunch. When I returned, Ben Luper was in my waiting room. He was about fifty, gray-haired, dark-suited, and all business. We shook hands and I showed him into my office. I gave him Ant's documents, and he took a seat in one of my customer chairs and looked the papers over while I sat behind my desk, twirled my hat around my finger, and smoked a cigarette.

"They're records of financial transactions all right," Luper said. "But how do you know they're from McGahee? I don't see his name anywhere."

"Damn, I forgot to get an affidavit," I said sarcastically. "But you got my word."

"You think somebody took these pages from one of McGahee's ledgers?"

"One of his former employees, you know, the dead guy," I replied. Luper pushed back his fedora and studied the papers again. I twirled my hat some more. He shuffled the papers some more. Then he finally looked over at me.

"Maybe these are legit, or maybe somebody's trying to set up the old man," he said. "Look, McGahee's an investment banker, and these records appear to show how much money some of his customers invested with his firm. I've done some dabbling in the stock market. Typically, brokers like McGahee trade stocks and bonds for their investors. But my guess is he wasn't buying or selling any stocks for these clients. Let me show you something." He walked over and plunked down the documents on my desk. I snuffed out my cigarette and pushed my ashtray, piled high with spent butts, to the side.

I watched as he moved a long finger across one of the pages. There were two headings: INVESTMENTS and DIVIDENDS. Names, dates, and dollar amounts were entered in rows underneath. I could feel a headache coming on.

"These records are from several years ago," Luper said. "I bet most of his investors are in it for the long haul anyway. They're probably older people, like McGahee, and they want to fatten up their retirement funds. Here, this entry indicates Alvin Jansen invested ten thousand." He tapped his finger on the paper. "And here's where his money apparently went. Two thousand was divided equally among these four gentlemen." He pointed to four names on the right-hand side of the page. The sum of five hundred dollars was entered next to each one. "McGahee was probably taking Jansen's money and paying dividends to other investors. Then you can see the balance of eight thousand was entered alongside two letters: ME. Could be ME stands for McGahee Enterprises. Or maybe McGahee's referring to himself. Either way, he was most likely depositing the eight grand in his bank account. Kind of looks like Mr. Jansen was being fleeced. If you look down the page, you'll see the same formula is repeated again and again with different customers and different sums. And a large chunk always goes to ME. Notice that Jansen's name is the only one underlined. Like someone wanted to draw attention to it."

Luper looked at me and smiled. Then he sorted out two neatly typed business forms from the bottom of the pile. "These are carbon copies of account statements presumably sent to a couple of McGahee's clients. I didn't notice them at first. McGahee's company name is at the top. The forms supposedly notify these clients of the value of their investments and any profits they've earned. I'll skip the financial jargon and round off the numbers. One statement shows A. Jansen owning nineteen hundred shares of American Galaxy worth ten grand. The other one tells us that J. Peterson's twelve hundred shares of New Vanguard earned him five hundred dollars in dividends. You may recall he was one of the four names I showed you on the right side of the ledger sheet."

Everything became hazy as I stared at the forms. My headache had finally arrived. I tilted back in my chair and rubbed my eyes.

"Let's assume the ledger sheets are authentic," he continued. "Then Mr. Jansen doesn't own any shares of American Galaxy, and Mr. Peterson's five hundred in profits didn't come from any investment in New Vanguard. Here's how I think McGahee's been working his con. Instead of investing the money of his new clients, he's offering some of it to prior clients as dividends and helping himself to the rest. My guess is he sends his customers fabricated account statements—just like these—to make everything look like it's on the up-and-up. His investors may think they're stockholders, but they don't own shit. I believe what we got here is a Ponzi scheme. He didn't even bother using a code to disguise it. Guess he wasn't worried about getting caught."

"Can you use these documents to bring down the old man's financial empire?" I tried not to betray my true feelings about the SOB.

"You really want to get this guy, don't you?" he said.

"Maybe he's guilty of more than just bilking his customers. You think it was a coincidence his employee was gunned down after he got wise to McGahee's scheme?" I tried my best to sound sincere. Framing McGahee for Ant's killing was about as likely as Ginger Rogers dancing a tango with me. But it was an enjoyable thought just the same. Even nailing him for financial fraud was probably a long shot.

"Who knows where a police investigation might lead?" Luper said. "I'll have our financial reporter take a look at these records. We'll have to verify they're from McGahee." I handed him Ant's envelope. He stuffed the papers inside. "Call me if you don't hear from me by five."

I gave him my card. "Make sure you keep my name out of it. Can't you say in your story that the documents came from McGahee's murdered employee?"

"We'll probably say we found them in our mailbox," he said. "That's what we ordinarily do when we don't want to reveal our source. Talk to you later."

As he exited, I took off my coat and planned on settling in for the afternoon, even though Fridays were usually short days for me. Vincent McGahee's number was still busy and I couldn't reach Nehemiah. I cranked some paper into my typewriter and killed time by working on some crime fiction. When I tried McGahee's number again, the butler picked up the phone.

"May I speak with Ashley Greene, please?"

"Who's calling?"

"Sid Craven. Before you hang up, Geoffrey, tell her I've got a potentially incriminating snapshot of two reckless lovebirds."

"I'm afraid I haven't a clue as to what you're alluding to."

"You're not supposed to. You're a servant. I'd relay the message if I were you and wanted to hang on to my cushy job." He followed my suggestion.

"Yes, Mr. Craven," Ashley said. "What is it you want *now*?"

"I'm holding a photo of a supposedly grieving couple in a shocking embrace. The police may be interested."

"I guess you're referring to the other day when Vincent and I were obviously comforting one another during a time of mourning for our beloved Simone. Only an insensitive misfit would intrude on such a private moment with a camera."

"If kissing and groping one another is your idea of mourning, you may want to consider obtaining the services of a good lawyer."

"That sounds like a cheap blackmail attempt to me," she said.

"I wouldn't call it cheap, Ashley. I'd say this picture's worth a thousand words and perhaps a thousand bucks. At any rate, that's a good starting point. Look at it this way. I'm conducting a private auction. If you don't give me a reasonable bid on my revealing photo, I'll call Bert Brenley at the *Mirror* to see if *he's* interested."

"Go ahead. *I'll* call the cops. Blackmail's a crime."

"What about homicide?"

"You must be joking. Even if your photo shows what you claim, what would it prove?"

"It may not *prove* anything, but it may *imply* a motive for murder. I'll give you until, say, five this afternoon before I call the *Mirror*. We need to talk in person. I'm at the Chandler Building on Olympic near Central. I'm on the tenth floor. Check the directory in the lobby. Good afternoon, Ashley."

After hanging up, I dialed the Charcoal, but Nehemiah hadn't shown up yet. So I left a message for him to call me at my office. While waiting, I continued on my detective story. Maybe my writer's block was finally gone. I hadn't tossed out any pages lately.

Luper called about four. "The documents appear to be legitimate," he said. "We looked up a number of the old man's customers in the phone book. We reached a dozen people. Some wouldn't talk to us. But others acknowledged being McGahee's clients. Most said they chose to have their profits reinvested instead of receiving cash payouts. Naturally, they were concerned about their investments. We couldn't get hold of McGahee himself."

"You gonna try to get the story in tomorrow's paper?" I asked.

"We've got more phone calls to make and more facts to check. We don't want a lawsuit on our hands. We may even talk to the IRS about McGahee. You know, tell them we acquired documents showing some of his 1940 financial dealings and suggest they might want to compare them with his reported income for that year. Could be he's guilty of tax evasion. It's worth a shot. That's how they got Al Capone. I don't know what we can actually prove, but sometimes you just got to go with your instinct on a story. You know, roll the dice. When the news gets out about McGahee's banking habits, his customers will want to know what's going on with their funds. Even if he's able to dodge our allegations, his clients might panic. That could lead to a run on his bank."

"Can't wait to hear how the old man tries to explain where all that money went," I said with a snicker. "How could he have flimflammed everyone for so long?"

"I don't know. People are gullible. And McGahee's built up a reputation as a smart and trustworthy investor. You saw how he was distributing the money. He's probably been stringing along his investors by offering them sizable payouts. But one of his employees evidently got access to his private accounting books. Our financial guy here says McGahee undoubtedly keeps another set of books for when he gets audited. That's where he would record phantom investments in stocks. Who knows how he keeps track of everything? That's what he has accountants for."

"Sounds like there's a good chance the old man's going down," I said hopefully. He agreed and we hung up. I wouldn't be content until I saw a newspaper photo of McGahee being led away in handcuffs.

THIRTY-FIVE

At five I opened my desk drawer and—for the first time today—took out the office bottle. Empty. It had been a long week. I felt as worn out as a hunk of chewing gum stuck to the bottom of a shoe. I put on my suit coat, which was already getting a rumpled look. Before making a run to the liquor store, I decided to type a short note for Ashley in case she showed up during my absence. I'd stick it on my office door. I scrolled a blank sheet into my Underwood and quickly typed her name and a message aimed at catching her attention.

When I heard the buzzer, I yanked out the paper, balled it up, and heaved it towards the wastebasket. My errant toss hit the front of my filing cabinet and rolled into the center of the room. A rare miss, but I didn't believe in omens. I pushed my typewriter out of the way, opened one of my desk drawers, and dropped my partial detective story and today's *Times* inside. I was ready when my visitor knocked on the office door.

As I stood up, a woman dressed for mourning strolled through the doorway. Pausing in front of the crumpled paper on the floor, she bent down, picked it up with her left hand and flipped it easily into my wastebasket. It rattled around inside the empty container. The usual heap of wadded-up detective fiction had been dumped out by the janitor.

"Shall we discuss your photo, Mr. Craven?" She sat in a customer chair and crossed her legs. Her stockings, shoes, purse, dress, and hat, with the veil lowered, were all black.

"Hello, Ashley." I sat down again. "Let me guess. You're supposed to be in mourning. I'm not buying it."

"Let's cut to the chase," she said bluntly. "Would you care to show me the photo in question?" I reached into my desk drawer and took out Simone's glossy publicity photo, the one for the recruitment drive. I held it so Ashley could see only the back of the picture.

"You're left-handed, aren't you, ma'am?" I asked.

"Guilty. Don't tell me that's a trick question and my answer just sealed my fate."

"Possibly. Simone was right-handed, wasn't she?" While Ashley paused—perhaps thinking it over—I glanced down at the picture I was holding. Simone was using her right hand to sign up with Uncle Sam. At Muriel's I'd been slapped and kicked by a lefty.

"She was ambidextrous, Mr. Craven. Now where does that leave you?"

"What about her temperament? Did she have a short fuse like you?"

"What the *hell* are you talking about, you damn dime store detective?" Her angry voice sounded familiar. Too familiar.

"Actually I believe I'm just an ordinary dime detective. But if I solve this case, maybe I'll get a promotion."

"Are you gonna show me the photo or are you just gonna waste my time?"

"The last time you saw Simone was Thursday. Two weeks ago. Right?"

"I already told you."

"Why do you think she turned up the next afternoon at Muriel's and caused such a commotion, Ashley?"

"Alcoholics are unpredictable, Mr. Craven. You, of all people, should know that."

I disregarded her cheap shot. "It was sure lucky for you she resurfaced on Friday."

"Why's that?" she said.

"She skips work," I said, "but then shows up at Muriel's. Now if she got drunk and drove off some canyon road shortly after tangling with me at the clothing store, she must have had a relapse of some sort. You and your lover certainly couldn't have arranged for her demise, since you were home at the time she supposedly crashed her car. But, of course, I never encountered Simone at Muriel's on Friday. She was already dead by then. You killed your sister Thursday night. It fits the coroner's time frame. He said Simone died sometime between Thursday night and Friday afternoon. I rechecked to make sure. You impersonated your sister to mislead the police. They assumed she was still alive Friday afternoon. That was some performance. But the part when you ripped open your blouse was a little over the top. However, I did enjoy the view. Guess the acting bug runs in the family."

Under her veil, Ashley raised her eyebrows and a smile briefly flickered on her lips. "Obviously the strain you've been under the past two weeks has corroded some of your brain cells," she said. "I doubt if logic was ever one of your strong points anyway. I was at a beauty salon in Hollywood when you had your run-in with my sister. The police already checked it out."

"You just buttoned up your blouse and drove over to the beauty parlor *after* leaving Muriel's. You even had a free umbrella to keep you dry when you stepped out into the rainstorm. Maybe you were late for your appointment, but who's gonna remember? You wanted to account for your whereabouts during your absence from the Beverly Glen house, since you were gone at the same time your sister was supposedly at Muriel's. But you didn't have to worry. The cops had no idea what you were up to." I reached for my Chesterfields, but I was out. I crumpled up the empty pack and dropped it on my desk. "Got a cigarette?" I asked her. She dismissed my question with a flick of her hand. I looked in my ashtray for a butt long enough to light up but couldn't find one.

"Old man McGahee's got clout with city hall," I continued. "So the cops got persuaded right off the bat not to make waves. The investigation into your sister's disappearance and then into her death got conveniently sidetracked. The old guy was just trying to protect his business. I figure he didn't realize he was also helping you and lover boy avoid the scrutiny that might have brought you to justice."

"You got some imagination," she said. "You should stick exclusively to crime fiction."

"I've heard that crack before. What about Miss Hicks, your neighbor in Frisco? What about *her* imagination? She seems to remember Vincent visiting you while he was on furlough."

"She's a stroke victim with a memory about as reliable as that junkyard car you drive."

"Simone's agent Harrison Hammerman got a call from your sister on the Thursday night before she vanished. Guess you didn't know Simone told him she discovered you and the war hero just banging away."

I stopped when I noticed the silver gun in Ashley's hand. She had taken it from her purse. The gun looked like a .25-caliber automatic. A small but potentially lethal weapon, it had to be the gun Nehemiah bought for Simone. Now it was pointed straight at my heart.

It was after five on a Friday, and the building was probably almost empty. Virtually no one would be around to hear a gunshot that most likely wouldn't be much louder than the sound of Wanda's secretary hitting a key on her typewriter. With her veil down, Ashley could make a clean getaway. The old security guard in the lobby would probably trip over himself opening the door for her.

"I'm not worried about some Hollywood pimp," she said with a hiss. "Let's see the photo, peeper."

I tossed it at her and got ready to make my move. She lifted up her veil and—careful to keep the gun aimed at me—set her purse on the floor. Then she leaned over and scooped up the picture. I got a good look at Ashley for the first time since we'd met at Muriel's. As she studied Simone's publicity photo, I noted her close resemblance to her sister. Ashley may have been better looking, but she was about as delightful as a broken collarbone.

"I knew you were bluffing, you bastard." She licked her lips and grinned. "This old photo was supposed to be a dead end. Who knew you'd be able to use it to track down those dopey starlets? We figured the strangler had a better chance of getting to them before you did."

"The photo of you and lover boy is locked in my file cabinet," I said offhandedly.

"You're full of it. There *is* no picture. That was just a ploy to get me over here. You're starting to get under my skin, snooper." Ashley angrily threw the publicity photograph onto the floor, and it sailed under my desk. "You know, we underestimated you."

She shook her head, and then she started talking. "I was fortunate as hell you were working undercover at Muriel's that Friday, because you turned out to be such a bungler. Who else would draw so much attention to a shoplifter? Which was exactly what we wanted. All those witnesses said they saw Simone at the store alive and well. Then I got Vincent to hire you to investigate her disappearance. I told him you could be manipulated as easily as one of Muriel's mannequins." As she rambled on, I ever so slowly rolled my chair away from my desk and prepared to make a play for her gun.

"We hired you to buy time," she explained. "You were our excuse for not notifying the police. We called you because we didn't want Simone's body found too soon. We wanted to make sure the coroner couldn't pin down the time of death. What we wanted was a quiet investigation that went nowhere. Within two days, however, your antics landed the story on the front page of the *Mirror*. And the police got involved. Turned out the body was already in the morgue." Ashley laughed. "When Vincent finally fired your ass, you wouldn't go away. You had to keep nosing around."

"You didn't show up on Beverly Glen to help Simone cope," I said. "She never called you. You showed up to help her husband get rid of her. The murder was premeditated, wasn't it?"

"Yeah, but the timing was a little off. We planned on waiting another week. But then fate stepped in. When Simone got back from the studio that Thursday, she walked right in on us. So I had to improvise. I think you'll admit that the murder weapon I chose was quite fitting for a B-movie queen. I crowned her with some B.S. acting trophy she won at college. I hit her so hard it must have cracked her skull. She'd flown into a rage after catching Vincent and me in the act. Said she was going to get a divorce lawyer and make Vincent pay big time. Simone kept talking about finally having proof. She wouldn't shut up. Then she became despondent and started crying. Just a typical mood swing for Simone. She started drinking, and after a while she calmed down. Then we heard her on the phone. She wasn't making much sense. Just jabbering away. But if someone believed her ramblings about me and Vincent, it would ruin our plans. I didn't know what else to do. So I grabbed her trophy, knocked the daylights out of her and then hung up the phone. She never saw it coming."

"That was her agent on the line. He knows about you and Vincent. You gonna kill him, too?"

"He didn't work it all out like you did. I've waited for two and a half years, and nobody's gonna spoil it now. I seduced Vincent on their honeymoon. Ever since then, Simone's days have been numbered. While she was living the high life on Beverly Glen, I was struggling just to get by. She was just lucky the war got in the way."

"Why'd you have to kill her?" I asked Ashley.

"A public divorce was out of the question. Nothing's more scandalous than a messy Hollywood breakup. The old man has a phobia about publicity. Out of spite, he probably would have cut off Vincent's allowance and taken him out of his will. We would've had each other but no inheritance. We couldn't take that chance."

"You know what?" I said. "Maybe the old man's got a notion who killed his daughter-in-law. But he doesn't care just as long as he can hush it up. I'm sure he's glad Simone's out of the way. She was a royal pain in the ass. Why didn't Vincent just talk his father into paying off Simone to get a quick Reno divorce? No publicity. It happens all the time."

"Not if you're a celebrity. Divorces always get leaked to the press. The old man would have nixed the idea anyway. He was too cheap to give Simone all the money she would've wanted. She got used to a life of luxury ever since she married into the McGahee family."

I decided to change the topic. "Did you know Simone had an insurance policy with Uptowner Life? It was part of her movie deal."

"Vincent already called her studio. They told him to get in touch with Uptowner. He probably just needs to come in and sign some forms. We got thirty grand coming our way."

"Don't count on it. Uptowner's gonna contend her death was a suicide, and that would disqualify Vincent's claim."

"The coroner said it could just as easily have been an accident," she said with a smile. "We've checked all the angles. We'll just sue Uptowner."

"Good luck. But that's peanuts compared to what you're really after. Just how do you plan on getting your greedy hands on the old man's millions?"

"Easy. After an appropriate period of mourning, I simply marry Vincent. It's only natural that we fall in love during our time of grief together. The old man's got a weak heart. And he's screwing his secretary, some dimwit who probably thinks a typewriter works like a player piano. He won't last long. We'll inherit everything. And we deserve it. You know, the old man forced Vincent to join the Army. He threatened to disown him if Vincent didn't enlist. He could have used his influence to get his son a deferment.

The old man could've gotten him a cushy banking job. But no! All that time wasted in the Army. We could have been together. Victor figured a son in the military would be good for business. He wanted everyone to see he was a patriotic American, whose son would volunteer to join up. Vincent wasn't gonna be one of those rich draft dodgers. And when he came back a war hero, the old phony notified the press to make sure the story made the front pages of the L.A. papers." She stopped and took a breath. Her gun was pointed my way when she started her rant, and it never wavered.

"Hey, Ashley, your gun's not loaded," I said, attempting to distract her.

"Nice try, but I loaded it myself," she retorted. "Found the gun and a box of cartridges in Simone's closet."

"How'd you get Simone's body and her car to the scene of the crash?"

"Vincent put her in the trunk of her own car. Then he drove the Packard while I followed in the Buick. We'd been planning it, so we knew exactly what to do. It was after midnight on Thursday, and there was absolutely zero traffic when we finally pulled the cars off the road at the edge of some forsaken canyon in the middle of nowhere. Vincent got out, and I rammed Simone's Packard with the big Buick and over it went. They didn't find her body for days."

"If she was in the trunk, how did her body get thrown clear of the wreck?"

"Vincent got out the tire iron and broke the lock so the trunk wouldn't slam shut on the way down. Her body bounced out just like we thought it would. We wanted her out in the open. We figured the coyotes would take her apart. Maybe all that rain kept them away. When I went downtown to ID Simone, her body was hardly mangled. Anyway, the coroner could only guess at the time of death."

"You two were taking a big chance."

"Life is just a gamble," she said with a wink. "Sometimes you gotta gamble if you want to win. Her car even caught on fire, but no one was around to notice it burn."

"Vincent's been extremely active for an invalid. He said his legs were paralyzed."

"It was the perfect hoax. How can you kill your wife if you're confined to a wheelchair?"

"I bet he didn't lose any toes either. Was that a lie, too?"

"He lost one toe," she said with a laugh.

"Man, what a bullshitter. He told me he lost a *number* of his toes."

"Hey, *one's* a number."

"What about your sister's drinking binges?"

"Another one of Vincent's whoppers," she said, shaking her head. "Simone had a reputation as a serious drinker. I know she liked to down a couple when she got downhearted. But the old man said she got religion and gave up drinking all together. I didn't believe it. But she stayed on the wagon the whole time after Vincent came home."

"What was Simone's reaction when *you* arrived on the scene?"

"We'd been on the outs for about a year. I figured she suspected Vincent was cheating on her. Whenever I talked to her on the phone, I could tell she was ticked off. So she gave me the cold shoulder. Vincent, too. She hardly talked to us. But my sister wasn't home much. Simone spent most days on casting calls. She was determined to restart her movie career. She finally called Victor for help. The old man knew a Hollywood agent with the right connections. That's how she landed a movie part." Ashley paused and sighed. "Simone was ready to make a comeback. The only time we saw her get drunk was the last night of her life. But we told the police she went on drinking binges. They just assumed it was true because of her reputation. Of course, drunks are reckless drivers, and they sometimes have fatal accidents."

"Vincent lied about Simone's history of shoplifting and tantrums, didn't he?"

"All made up to fit our story. We wanted her to look unstable."

"You framed your own sister after you killed her."

"And it worked—with your help."

"Think you're gonna get away with it, don't you?"

"Who's gonna stop me?" she said with a snort. "Not you, gumshoe."

"Did you know the old man's swindling his investors?" I asked, just for fun.

"Nothing would surprise me about that son of a bitch." She laughed.

"How about this? He's been running a Ponzi scheme. When it comes to your big inheritance, the joke's on you."

"You don't know what you're talking about."

I didn't feel like explaining it to her. She wouldn't believe me anyway. So, instead I asked her another question. "Did you know Bert Brenley was blackmailing Simone?"

"What do you mean?" she said.

"Maybe Victor was cheap, but he was paying hush money to Brenley." I quickly jumped to another topic. "Bet you didn't know Simone was a heroin addict. Did you know the old man had her committed to a private hospital? She was getting treatment at the same time Vincent was supposedly recuperating from his war injuries overseas."

"You're just making shit up," Ashley said. "You're trying to confuse me, you bastard. But it's not working." Despite her denial, she looked flustered.

"The old man was actually trying to save your sister while you were planning to do her in," I continued. "There's just a ton of stuff you and your boyfriend didn't know about Simone. She was good at keeping secrets when she wanted to. Looks like everybody in your family was hiding something."

They all had pieces of the puzzle. Just like everyone else I'd met on this case. But nobody had been able to put them all together. The last piece of *my* puzzle was in place, but I didn't like the picture. Thanks to carelessness or perhaps gravity, Ashley had been gradually lowering her gun until it was now pointing at the floor. I was about to spring from my chair, when the telephone rang. We both flinched. She jerked the gun up again, and I reached across my desk for the phone.

"Craven Investigations," I said into the mouthpiece.

"Sidney, it's Nehemiah. I'm returning your call."

Ashley stood up, walked over, and pressed her weapon against my side. She bent over and put her ear next to the phone.

"Can't talk now, man," I told him. "Got a visitor in the office."

"What have you found out about Simone?" he asked as Ashley started prodding me with her gun.

"I'm talking to her sister right now. Have to call you back later."

She snatched the phone from my grip and hung it up while managing to keep her gun jammed in my rib cage. "That was real clever!" she shrieked. "Now, who were you talking to?"

"Detective Drayton."

"Uh-uh. It sounded like—"

"Nehemiah Wright."

"Who?"

"Too bad you never found out. Maybe you could've blackmailed Simone, too."

"Found out about *what?*"

"Simone had been sleeping with a Negro bandleader. He even got her pregnant. She had an abortion. That's why Brenley was blackmailing her. I've been working for Simone's old boyfriend. Nehemiah wanted to find out what happened to your sister. Guess he really loved her. But he couldn't save her. Not from all the predators, not even from herself. He was right about her. She wasn't a quitter. But she made mistakes. Her last mistake was turning her back on you. Anyway, now he knows you're in my office. That was him on the phone. If you shoot me now, he'll finger you. Might as well give up."

Frowning, Ashley looked confused as she took a couple of steps backwards. She was within easy striking distance. Perhaps she was contemplating the ramifications of Nehemiah's phone call, figuring an angle, plotting her next move. I wasn't a mind reader. But I knew it was now or never. I didn't stop to consider the odds.

Then the buzzer went off. Ashley turned her head in the direction of my waiting room. I lunged from my chair and took a swipe at her little gun. When I swatted it from her hand, she screamed and jumped back. I stumbled past her and went crashing into one of my filing cabinets. Her weapon skittered across the carpet, coming to a stop at the feet of Bert Brenley, who had just opened the office door.

When the reporter, sporting a neck brace, awkwardly stooped down to pick up the gun, Ashley grabbed her purse and dashed for the doorway. She squeezed by Brenley and into the waiting room. I could hear her high heels reverberating down the corridor as Brenley pointed the little gun in my direction and struggled to stand up. He kept the gun trained on me and started walking my way. I held up my hands and backed away from the filing cabinets.

"What're you doing, Brenley?"

"I'll give you one guess."

"You injured your neck when your chair toppled over. You're pissed off and you wanna get even. Send me the doctor bill. Come on, put the gun down. We can talk this over."

"Under the circumstances I don't have time for any discussion." He plodded forward, backing me up until I bumped into the edge of my desk. Stopping a few feet away, Brenley used his sleeve to wipe the sweat from his forehead. "Looks like I'm not the only one with a grievance against you." He waved Ashley's weapon. "How convenient. Now I don't have to use my *own* piece. And that flighty dame will most likely take the blame."

"You know all that stuff you told me the other night," I said in a shaky voice. "I got a short memory. I've already forgotten almost everything. By tomorrow I guarantee you I won't remember anything."

I guess he didn't believe me. He took aim and shot me in the forehead. The noise sounded like a firecracker, but I went sprawling across the top of my desk just the same. I missed my typewriter but flattened my hat. My ashtray full of butts went flying. My shoulder hit the phone and knocked the receiver off the hook and over the edge of the desk.

"You shouldn't have embarrassed me in front of all those people." Brenley reached up and adjusted his neck brace. "I don't appreciate being subjected to public ridicule." He shoved the gun into his pocket, tried in vain to straighten his lopsided tie and then—whistling a catchy tune— casually swaggered from the office.

After getting to my feet, I began stumbling around aimlessly. I bumped into one of my customer chairs and knocked over the smoking stand. I couldn't decide whether to follow Brenley or to phone the police. The dial tone from the dangling receiver sounded far away. The office reeked of cordite. My vision was blurry, and my head was throbbing. I touched my forehead. It wasn't much of a hole, and hardly any blood.

I was a reasonably tough guy. I'd been through plenty the last two weeks. This was just one more setback. Feeling better already, I took another step and crumpled to the floor like a discarded page from one of my half-baked crime stories.

THIRTY-SIX

At about 2 A.M., the Chandler Building's chief custodian—making his rounds—discovered my body. He used my office phone to report the crime and then filched a twenty from my wallet before he went downstairs to await the police. He returned a short time later with three uniformed cops. Then Detective Drayton arrived with the ME and the rest of the homicide boys, and they were soon examining the corpse and searching my office for evidence.

"Hey, detective, who do you think shot the poor bastard?" asked Bert Brenley, resting against the wall just inside the office doorway, where he had a good view of the body. The fat reporter, his neck brace in place, had bribed a cop in order to get his second look at the crime scene. He was exhausted after climbing the fire stairs to the tenth floor.

"Who the hell let you up here?" Drayton said roughly.

"The officer downstairs said it was okay. I'm Brenley with the *Mirror*. Remember, we talked on the phone. I tipped you off about the Pearson dame's disappearance way back when. I was on my way home. Just happened to be driving by when I saw all the commotion." Brenley wiped his sweaty face with his handkerchief and eyed the fingerprint man, who was lifting prints off the door handle. Perhaps he was wondering if he might have left *his* prints. On his previous visit, he had neglected to wipe clean the door handles. Such carelessness might eventually cost him.

"You got good timing, Brenley," said Drayton, sighing heavily. "You're up here now. Might as well stay. Besides, I owe you one."

"Appreciate it." The reporter had already taken out a pencil and notebook from his suit coat. He was definitely curious to learn about whatever evidence the detective had uncovered.

"I get a kick out of your stuff, Brenley. It's just sleazy enough to keep me reading. I enjoyed your piece on the Dime Detective here. You must of ticked him off with your account of how he got his butt kicked by the Pearson frail at that ritzy clothing store." Drayton looked at Brenley and laughed. "Let me see if I can guess how you got that brace. He tried to wring your neck. But did you have to shoot him? Can't figure out what the two of you were doing in his office. But now you made the mistake of returning to the scene of the crime." Drayton laughed again. His attempt at a comic narrative was probably as close as he'd ever get to the truth.

"Sorry to disappoint you, detective," said Brenley, cracking a fake smile. "But this is just an old neck injury that acts up every now and then. Nothing serious." Considering the situation, the reporter seemed relatively calm. But he was sweating more than usual, if that was possible.

"Anyway, your story was good for a chuckle. But you could of mentioned *my* name more."

"An oversight on my part, detective."

"Just make sure I get more space this time."

"It can be arranged. Any suspects?"

"Anyone could of killed Craven. We already have *some* evidence. We'll know more when the lab results come in, right, Doc?" Drayton asked the ME, who had just taken my flattened fedora off the desk.

"That's right," he replied wearily. After punching my hat back into shape, he bent down and gently placed it over my face. "Now he's got some privacy. Besides, his eyes were giving me the creeps. My job's done for tonight. See you boys later." The ME, who had been chain-smoking since his arrival, flipped his cigarette butt into my wastebasket and then reached into his suit coat for another smoke. As he departed, Drayton waved at him. The sound of his coughing echoed down the hallway.

"Tell me, detective, was Craven still investigating Simone Pearson's death?" Brenley asked.

"Looks that way. I found a publicity photo of the actress under his desk. For what it's worth, there's some pretty clear thumbprints on it. Take a look at this." Drayton held up a pencil. A shell casing was dangling from the pencil point. "It's from a .25-caliber bullet. We lift prints off this casing, and we may be able to identify who loaded the murder weapon. The Pearson case is supposed to be officially closed. But guess what? It might just get reopened now."

"Think so?"

"Craven's murder definitely raises new questions about the case," Drayton said.

"Think he got bumped because he knew too much? I mean, did the Dime Detective somehow manage to figure out who killed the Pearson dame?"

"Who knows? But the wheels downtown might not be able to keep a lid on it anymore. Maybe I'll finally get a chance to solve the damn thing. Could be we find Craven's murderer, we unravel the Pearson case."

"What wheels?"

"No comment," said Drayton, frowning.

"A front-page headline in the *Mirror* might create enough publicity to nudge the department into taking action," Brenley said. "Could mean a step up for some smart detective." Maybe Brenley wasn't worried that a renewed police investigation into the case might expose his blackmail scheme. Maybe he figured he was safe because the only eyewitnesses, Simone and Ant, were dead. Maybe he was confident he could outsmart Drayton and get away with murder. Maybe his pursuit of a big scoop blurred his judgment. Maybe I was thinking too much.

"Hey, Brenley, you hear we nabbed the Starlet Strangler?" Drayton asked.

"When? I've been working day and night on that story."

"About two hours ago. Got some more details on the police radio coming over here. You were probably out gallivanting around town."

"It's Friday night. What do you expect? I've busted my ass all week. I'm entitled to a little recreation once in a while, and I'm not gonna let this neck brace slow me down. Tell me how you caught the strangler."

"Remember the starlet that got away?" Drayton asked. Brenley winced as he tried to nod his head. The detective smiled. "She gave us an excellent description of the killer."

"You know, the *Mirror* ran a police drawing of the suspect on the front page along with *my* detailed report on the girl's close encounter with him," Brenley said, gloating.

"That's how we got him. We got a tip from some dame. Turns out she's the strangler's wife. Said she found out the killer's identity from your tabloid. Guess it scared the hell out of her when she realized she was married to a lunatic. Looks like she'll get the fifty-grand reward."

"Know anything about the guy they caught?"

"He was a night watchman in Hollywood. Police surrounded the warehouse he was supposed to be guarding. They found him drunk and passed out on the job. And his shift had just started. It still took a dozen cops to subdue the screwy fucker. Some of 'em wound up in the hospital."

Brenley was busy taking notes. "What's his name?"

"Can't recall. He was an ex-stuntman at one of the studios. He knew his way around. Guess he'd just follow an actress home when she left for the day." Drayton looked around the room. "Anybody know the name of the guy they arrested? The strangler?"

The fingerprint man and the photographer were taking a smoke break over by the filing cabinets. They both shook their heads.

"Watkins!" Drayton snapped his fingers. "No, just a minute. Wilkins. That's it. Wilkins. He was living with his wife in the Valley."

"That name sounds familiar," Brenley said, wrinkling his brow. His hand was shaking as he jotted down the name. "It's gotta be Ted Wilkins. His wife is Faye Fluellen. She was a starlet at Empire. Wonder if she was somewhere on his list."

"Well, she's safe now."

"Not to mention rich."

"I know this much. Somebody's getting a promotion out of it." Drayton walked over and opened my desk drawer. He found the Pearson file folder and started thumbing through it.

"Okay if I come in and check out the crime scene?" Brenley asked.

"I don't see any harm. Just don't get in the way." Then he pointed to the camera slung over the reporter's shoulder. "And no photos." Brenley wandered in and peeked over Drayton's shoulder. Undoubtedly, he wanted to get a look at my file to see if he was mentioned in it. Guess he'd been in too much of a hurry for any snooping when he stopped by earlier. My scribbles probably wouldn't help the cops or implicate Brenley in blackmail. I had kept most of my notes in my head.

"Can't even read his writing," Brenley complained as he started for the door. "I've got a busy night ahead of me with two breaking stories. Gotta get back to the office and make some phone calls. Maybe we'll run a special edition."

He stopped at my wastebasket when he noticed smoke drifting from it. "Looks like somebody dropped a lit butt in the trash can." Hampered by his unwieldy neck brace, Brenley slowly bent over, reached in, and brought out a smoldering, partly glowing wad of paper. He quickly dropped it on the floor. He stepped on the balled paper a couple of times, then squatted down and picked it up. The big man straightened up with a groan. As he unfolded the paper, ashes flaked off and floated to the floor.

"Got a clue there?" Drayton asked, chuckling. He walked over to take a look. Brenley smoothed out the paper on his leg and held it up for both of them to see. A corner was burned off the partly blackened page. The words were smudged but legible.

It was the note I had typed for Simone's sister. The last words I'd ever write: "Ashley. Won't be gone long. Really want to hear your confession. Don't start without me."

Of course, at the time I didn't have a clue I'd soon be gone for good. Maybe my note would point Drayton in the direction of Simone's killer. If he tracked down Ashley, she might get blamed for both murders. Then she would undoubtedly attempt to finger Brenley for *my* killing. She probably didn't know him by sight. But her description of him would be a dead giveaway: an obese guy wearing a baggy suit and a neck brace. Even Drayton would recognize the culprit, but he'd need evidence to arrest him.

Maybe the Chandler Building's security guard had glimpsed the fat reporter. Maybe his fingerprints were on my door handle. Maybe Faye Fluellen would blow the whistle on Brenley's blackmail scheme. One thing might lead to another, and Drayton might nab the SOB.

Ashley would probably make a deal with the D.A. The two lovers might be allowed to plead guilty to manslaughter and save the state the cost of a trial. Both Ashley and Vincent would be locked up for a long time. Even if

Ashley took the fall for Brenley's crime, the judge might exercise leniency in sentencing her. The state balked at executing women.

If the real culprit took the rap, however, he wouldn't be so lucky. I could just imagine the fat bastard sitting in the gas chamber and trying to hold his breath until his eyes bugged out, and then finally inhaling the cyanide fumes that would take his life.

I was counting on Drayton to get to the bottom of the whole mess. Perhaps I should have drawn a map to the Beverly Glen mansion. That would have given him a start in the right direction. Anyway, the case was out of my hands now.

ABOUT THE AUTHOR

After graduating with a journalism degree from California State University at Northridge, Hal Schick worked as an editor and writer in Los Angeles. Then he entered the College of Education at the University of Georgia and is now a school teacher in Athens, GA. He also works with Habitat for Humanity.